# HER HONOR'S BODYGUARD
## WRITTEN BY
### Johnny Ray
### Copyright © 2012
### SIR JOHN PUBLISHING
### ALL RIGHTS ARE HEREBY RESERVED
### BY THE AUTHOR JOHNNY RAY

Do first loves ever really die?

While reunions can take many forms, there is always one question that has to be answered sooner or later—what happened?

Vance had always been extremely proud of Noella, and just because his life had been ruined, he saw no reason why she had to have the same fate. When his dad died, leaving him and his mother penniless, he dropped out of law school and ended his relationship with Noella, but in doing so, he stopped a scandal that could have ruined her family. These secrets he would never let her know. Ironically, years later, he would have never guessed she would be instrumental in ruining his career with the Tampa police force.

After Noella finished law school and started pursuing her goal of working up the ranks in judgeships, she never considered inviting another guy into her life. As such, when someone attempts to threaten her into vacating her seat on the bench, and by force if necessary, she knows of no one else she really trusts as much as Vance, who now has a successful bodyguard and private detective business.

She knows that Vance might hate her for her part in having him dismissed from the police force, but what he will never know is that she actually saved him from going to prison. Additionally, she now thinks he was framed, and perhaps by the same people who are threatening her. She had to talk him into taking her on as a client . . . but would he agree to her request?

As the number of attacks on her life increases, Vance soon has no choice but to offer her his protection, and in spite of everything, when they see each other again their old attraction for each other returns. She wants the truth. He wants the truth. However, making the ultimate sacrifice is not always easy to understand, whether given or received. Ultimately . . . could they now trust each other with these secrets? While their lives depend on discovering the truth to their past, these truths are locked in deep secrets that could also destroy them.

**Johnny Ray** is an award winning novelist who won the Royal Palm literary award for best thriller and is quickly making a name for himself as the master of the romantic thriller. He loves social interaction with his readers and can be found on

Twitter

**www.twitter.com/sirjohn_writer**


Facebook

**www.facebook.com/authorjohnnyray**.


He can also be reached by e-mailing at

**sirjohnnyray@gmail.com**


Or you can just follow him on his blog at

**www.sirjohn.us**

for updates and future releases.

**Johnny Ray's additional novels:**

**LITERARY AGENT–BEWARE**

Published by Sir John Publishing in 2012

**SCANDAL–THE DEATH OF A LEGACY**

Published by Sir John Publishing in 2012

**MODELS AND LOVERS**

Published by Sir John Publishing in 2012

**A WAR HERO RETURNS**

Published by Sir John Publishing in 2013

**FOR LOVE AND VENGEANCE**

Published by Sir John Publishing in 2012

**THE SALSA CONNECTION**

Published by Sir John Publishing in 2012

**THE JOURNEY TO WHITESTONE**

Published by Sir John Publishing in 2012

**STALKING LOVE**

Published by Sir John Publishing in 2013


**JOHN RAIN –THE HAWAIIAN AFFAIR**

Published by Amazon digital 2013

# HER HONOR'S BODYGUARD

## BY

## JOHNNY RAY

## Chapter 1

*What in the hell am I supposed to do now*? Noella Peterson stopped walking along the street as she studied a car that was slowing while it passed by her. While hesitating, she had second thoughts in revealing where she was heading. Although she felt like she had eluded everyone, she couldn't be absolutely sure. She waited in the midday sun for the car to disappear quietly around a corner.

The office front of this older building near the college in downtown Tampa offered her little to use for cover. She inhaled deeply, hoping the door would be unlocked so that she could enter quickly and disappear before the car made a circle.

She studied the name on the window, which reassured her that she had the right place. Vance Mills, private detective, was about to obtain a new client. She twisted the polished, brass door knob and swiftly pushed the door open. Her heart raced as she rushed inside and closed the door behind her.

After studying the dimly lit waiting area, she waited for someone to notice that she had entered the office. She heard no music playing, or in fact any sounds at all to interrupt the pounding of her heart. After studying the deathly quiet sensation of the vacant office, she wondered if she should come back later. No, she had come this far.

A small light glowing above the desk, and another one on a table next to several chairs, sent additional quivers to her stomach. Still, with the lights left on, someone must be here.

"Is anyone here," she shouted, as the sparsely furnished room allowed her voice to echo. When she suddenly heard a bump coming from a side room, she realized that someone was there after all. She straightened her back and waited.

The door swung open and in walked Vance who was wearing gym shorts and a muscle type t-shirt. The sweat glistening on his skin highlighted his rock hard body. Damn, she knew she shouldn't stare, but he looked hot. As her heart raced, she refocused on his eyes which were attempting to make contact with hers.

After several long agonizing seconds, he pulled the door closed behind him. "Hello, Noella, or should I call you judge here also?"

"Vance, this isn't my courtroom, so you know you don't have to call me *judge*." This was difficult for her, and it appeared that he wanted to make the moment as tough as he could for her. "I need to talk to you. Vance, I need your help."

"My help?"

"I know you're mad at me, and for good reason. But . . . what you don't know is what I've recently found out. I highly suspect that you were framed."

Vance strolled over to his desk as she watched his movements. Memories of her making love to him many years ago resurfaced. He looked even better than she could remember.

If he thought he could turn on any kind of recording device—well, forget it. "I don't know. Maybe this was a bad idea." She hesitated, hunting for the right words. "But I remember you from back in law school. You were the one who always held the ethical high road, and I always respected that."

Vance pointed to a chair for her to use, but he remained silent. His solid black hair had become slightly longer over the last year, and it now reached closer to his shoulders. His deep, penetrating, almost wolf-like, grey eyes had retained their effectiveness in unsettling her.

She forced herself to speak slowly. "I need to hire a private detective to do some work for me and keep it quiet. I might also need some protective services, if you are available."

Vance motioned again for her to have a seat, but didn't wait for her as he slipped into his chair. "How did you find me? I don't advertise, and I take on only a select number of clients."

"I understand how you're keeping a low profile. You really made some enemies in the police department."

"Not everything is as it appears. I still have some friends there." He grabbed a towel, and wiped sweat from his neck. "You'll have to excuse me, I just started working out." He pointed to the side door. "My gym."

"It's good to see that you stay in shape—it shows." Perhaps she didn't need to make such a comment. The short fling they had earlier had ended years ago, and there was no sense in reuniting those memories now. But . . . how could she ignore his body that he flaunted in front of her?

"I'm sure there're many *competent* people you can work with around town."

As she allowed herself to breathe, the scent of his workout sweat reached her, making it harder to hide her emotions. She had to act professionally, she had to. "I've been getting threatening calls and messages."

He smirked. "That sounds like something you can turn over to the police."

"I have talked to them and I've gotten nowhere. The only comments that I have received from them is that maybe if I can't take the heat of being a judge that *just maybe* I should think about stepping down."

"How are you being contacted?"

"Phone calls with hang ups. People in the distance studying me. Cars following me. Nothing I can use to charge anyone with. It's as if they know the limits, and stay slightly outside them."

He hesitated this time before he asked, "Again . . . have you had any direct threats?"

"If I did, I could have better protection from the Tampa police and the state, but I don't. Vance, this is why I would like to hire you."

"You mentioned that you thought I was framed."

"Thinking and proving are two different things. Listen, we both know that I shouldn't be discussing this with you."

"As you probably remember, about a year ago I was advancing with the police department and getting close to obtaining funds for me to go back to law school. That was before you stepped in." His eyes refocused on her, and immediately increased the stress ravaging her body.

"I know, and I'm sorry. I'm sure that you think I'm the reason that you lost your job. What you don't know is that I'm the one who stopped you from being prosecuted."

"So you struck a deal without even consulting me."

"You know this can never leave this room."

Without acknowledging her comment, he

continued, "You mentioned that you have new evidence. Are you going to tell me what it is?"

"In time—yes. I came here because I thought I could trust you. If you don't want to help me, I understand. But . . . if that is the way you feel, I don't see any reason in telling you anymore details about what's happening to me."

He released his stare, his hold on her, as he glanced at a nearby wall for a second. "I would love to help you, but with all of the complications involved I need to do some serious thinking about it. Can I let you know in a day or two?"

"All I can tell you for now is that by helping me you might be helping yourself." Noella stood and glanced around at the shabby surroundings. She never dreamed he would crumble like this. Not with her own home hidden in one of the most exclusive and restrictive neighborhoods in Safety Harbor. Their lives had definitely changed for both of them.

"Do you have a cell phone that I can call you on?"

Noella reached for her phone. "I never call myself."

"Not a problem." Vance reached for his and

pressed a button. "I have it."

She felt stunned, and slightly violated. "Like that, you have my number!"

"Modern technology is good, or bad, depending on how you use it."

"This is scary." She turned toward the door. "Vance, I hope you consider helping me."

"It's not that I don't want to help." He refocused on her eyes. "I just need to think about the complications involved."

"Fair enough."

Vance appeared to weaken as he continued. "Until then. You'll also see my number on your phone. Call me if you do feel threatened. Listen, I'm sure this will pass. We both know you're not the *favorite little sister* for a lot of people."

"It comes with the job." She dropped her phone back into her pocket. "Thanks for your time."

He walked to the door, but hesitated before he spoke. "This isn't a really bad side of town, but if you want me to I can walk you to your car."

"Don't be silly. I'll be fine. I hope you'll call me." She wasn't sure when, but one day she would make it up to him for the damaged she had inflicted upon him. Still, with all of her doubt concerning the Tampa police department, she needed him. The police force had many dedicated officers, but she knew there were those inside that shouldn't be working there.

She turned to her left and began walking along the sidewalk. Her long days in the court had molded her into who she was. She studied her conservative suit, which she was sure made her look much older than she was. Becoming one of the youngest judges in history had created problems she never would have expected.

She glanced at her car, a BMW E4 convertible, which might not be as conservative as most judges would drive, but underneath she was still a woman with desires she had to live with. And these desires were suddenly burning with the thoughts of one fantastic hunk she had hoped to put behind her.

She had been warned many times as she stretched for her goal of becoming a judge. A state circuit judge was just the first step on her way up the ladder of judgeships.

As she walked, she glanced over her shoulder to study Vance, who, obviously, was patiently waiting on her. While he acted like he didn't care, she knew, or at least hoped, otherwise.

After walking almost half of the way to her BMW, she saw another car, a dark, dingy sedan of some kind pulling away from a curb. Should she wait until they passed and stay closer to Vance, or should she hurry to get safely inside her car?

The decision was taken from her when the car sped forward, and a guy jumped out of the back seat. She turned to run back toward Vance, who in turn, was now running full out toward her.

However, the guy from the car grabbed her before Vance made it to her. She watched Vance raise his hands and come to a stop. A glance over her shoulder revealed the reason why—a short, shotgun barrel was leveled at him from the sedan, which was now even with them.

The guy grabbing her increased his hold on her waist, and one breast. Vance might be facing down a gun barrel, but she wasn't. Her fingernails came to life as she lowered her hand to his crotch and dug in.

After the guy yelled, she felt him attempt to pull from her grip. Then the barrel of the shotgun shifted in her direction. With another quick glance to her right, she watched Vance quickly drop to one knee before retrieving a pistol from his ankle holster and fire. The car tires squealed as the driver hit the gas. Vance fired an additional three times before turning to the guy left behind.

The guy holding her released her, and reached for a pocket. As soon as he produced a gun, she heard an explosively loud shot, and watched her attacker's head jerk backwards. She turned her head, but it wasn't soon enough to avoid seeing the blood splatter from the back of his head.

As she began to stumble, her world went crazy with lights swirling around her. Seconds later, she felt arms grabbing her as she fell, and her world went black.

## Chapter 2

Vance shifted in his seat as Noella started to wake. "Easy, you're going to be fine." He felt so sorry for her.

"Where am I?"

"We're in an ambulance."

"Am I going to the hospital?" Noella tried to raise her head, but failed.

"I don't think so. They thought it would be better for you to rest here than on the street. How are you?"

"You …." She tried to raise her head again. "You shot someone!"

"Please, just relax." He gently placed a firm hand on her forehead to reassure her, and to stop her from attempting to raise her head again. "Yes, and that is another reason they wanted you to come inside here. It's not a pretty sight outside."

He watched her raise her hands to her face. "What do they want with me?"

"I don't know. I'll have to go file a report and answer some questions soon, but since you'll have a police escort, you'll be fine."

"No! You don't understand. I'm staying with you."

Stopping her appeared to be impossible. She obviously knew much more about what was going on. "Okay, but since you witnessed what went down I'm sure they'll have questions for you also."

"What about the guys in the car?"

"They got away, but the police have a massive man hunt after them now." He watched her close her eyes, as he continued to wonder what she had gotten involved in. Like it or not, he needed to help her.

Detective Nelson knocked on the side of the door as he stepped inside. Vance had always trusted him before, but with the words of Noella sounding alarms, he decided to take a wait and see approach.

Nelson passed a quick smile his way before speaking loud enough for all to hear. "Do we need to take you to the hospital, or will you be okay, judge?"

She forced herself to gain control, to act professional. "I'll be fine. Who are these people?"

"The guy Vance shot has no identification on him. It may take a while to get an ID on him. He appears to be a mixture of Latino and Spanish, but who knows for sure. It will take a little longer to gather the crime scene data."

"What about the ones who got away?"

"We're still hunting for them." He turned toward Vance. "Are you sure you hit him?"

"The first shot—definitely. The next three, I'm not so sure. Since the windows were tinted, I have no idea how many were inside. Obviously they had a driver."

"You said you saw a gun barrel, but never heard a shot."

"After the barrel shifted toward the judge, I fired first. When the driver hit the gas, I fired several more rapid shots. It would be hard to say for sure if he fired, or not. However, I don't think so."

Noella asserted herself. "I saw the gun, but I don't remember hearing it fire."

"Chances are we'll find the car soon, and if the guys are shot they'll show up in a hospital somewhere later." Nelson patted his leg and motioned to the door.

"You can both ride with me if you want."

Vance considered the request, but hesitated. "Since we'll need a ride home, I can bring the judge with me."

"Are you going to be providing her with protection?" Nelson waited on an answer.

The question from Nelson forced him to make a decision that he had not totally agreed to—yet. Vance knew he couldn't disclose that they were previous lovers, or even begin to try to explain why she had him removed from the force. At the same time, he didn't want to explain why Noella came to him for protection. "It's up to her. I was just offering my services, since I'll be coming back this way anyway."

Noella appeared to understand the situation, as she spoke quickly in Vance's defense. "I would appreciate the ride, and in light of this, I really might need some private security. We do need to talk."

Nelson stood and stretched out his hand. "I hate to ask for it, but you know I'll need the gun you used as evidence until this case is resolved."

"I was wondering when you would be asking for it." He leaned over and retrieved the forty-five snub nose from his ankle holster. "Take good care of it. Not many small guns have this kind of power."

Nelson accepted the gun, and glanced at the opening in the barrel. "What is this?"

"A forty five magnum."

"Wow, something this powerful and short can't be accurate for any distance at all. And you carry it in your ankle holster?" He shook his head. "I don't even want to know what else you carry."

"It was never designed for accuracy, but for fire power up close when you need it."

"You know that using excessive force is what got you kicked off the force?"

"Nelson, what you call excessive force is what has kept me alive."

Vance watched Nelson glance over at Noella—the meaning all too clear. This would be better discussed elsewhere. "We need to get together to catch upon old times one day."

Vance glanced away as he replied. "I look forward to it." While he knew he needed to maintain contacts inside the force, trusting anyone would be hard to do.

Noella waited for Nelson to leave. "Thanks for keeping this quiet."

"Yeah, thank me later. We need to talk."

"Yes we do. People will want to know why I came to see you. What are you going to tell them?"

"Client privilege. I don't have to tell them anything."

While he obviously knew the law, she was glad he understood the situation. "While you, without doubt, will be found justifiable in shooting this, or these guys, you'll be placed under extensive questioning. Do you have an attorney?"

"No money for one, and I don't think I'll need one." Perhaps he felt slightly cocky, but he knew the law well. He would have made a good lawyer, if only .

. . .

Images of the guy's head exploding and sending blood everywhere returned. A forty-five magnum bullet was powerful. While she knew that, this was the first time she had ever actually witnessed someone being shot or killed. Despite her intentions to hold her nerves together, her body started to quiver. This would be a good time for a shot of tequila, a habit she had obtained on a trip, or two to Mexico.

She felt a hand on her shoulder, breaking her free of the haunting images. However, she knew she would be put through it several times during the next few hours, as she would have to give statements.

"Are you okay?" he asked.

Was he really concerned about her, or just being nice? "Yes and no. Someone just tried to kidnap me—damn it! You have to believe me, someone is after me. Vance, you have to help me find out why."

She watched him soften his cold exterior around him, as if for the first time. "You definitely made your case, but I'm still not convinced I'm the best person to help you."

"How well do you know Nelson?" This seemed like the best place to start. Many of the names that she was suspicious of she would have to wait until later to discuss, and only if she could even do it then. She knew that she was skating on very thin ice, to use an old cliché, or even better, on a very slippery slope.

"We were preparing to become partners when I was asked to leave the department."

"I didn't know that." *An interesting twist*. But exactly how much did Vance trust Nelson? And, more importantly, who did Vance really trust? She suspected he had others in the force that he still talked to.

"Don't worry about it. What was done is history now." He pointed to the door again. "We need to be going. I'm not sure exactly what you'll see on the outside. Are you ready for this?"

"Not really, but I don't have much choice, do I?"

He opened the door and turned to help her with the tall step, as her dress rose slightly in the process. She noticed the stare, and the slight twitch in his smile. Their history appeared to be ancient, but in that moment it sprang forward. Well . . . at least for her it did.

While holding her arm, he moved her quickly to one side, and away from the main center of attention. Police tape marked the area. A dozen or so police cars had their blue lights flashing, as many police officers and plainclothesmen walked around. While several chalk lines had been drawn on the pavement, thankfully no dead body was insight. Had it already been moved, or was it simply covered?

After reaching the sidewalk, Vance turned her in the opposite direction of her car. Moments later, he directed her into a small parking lot where his large, black truck was parked. She should have known.

"The seat is high. I'm sorry about that."

He opened the door. *Damn, he didn't lie. How in the hell am I going to climb into this?* She started to change her mind and drive herself. "I don't think I've ever been in a monster truck before."

"Well . . . there's a first for everything. Here is a step you can use, and it's not near as bad as you think."

Maybe so, but the chances of her showing more leg this time was obvious. She twisted away from him to make sure he didn't see too much skin. Surprisingly, he was right as she climbed easily into the seat before he closed the door behind her.

As she waited for him to join her in the cab, she glanced around. It looked like a modern cockpit in a fighter jet with a large GPS screen, a computer console, and several compartments with closed doors.

Vance stepped into the cab, and cranked the motor

in one motion. "You need to buckle up." He smiled, as he fastened his own.

"This is an impressive set up. Did you have this custom built?"

"No. I managed to find it online for sale in Chicago."

"Really?" She wondered how he could afford such a truck. She knew his financial situation from earlier. Life had to be hard on him when his dad died and left him and his mom near poverty. He had shown so much promise in law school until then. When he had to drop out of school, he had also disappeared out of her life.

Vance leaned over, and opened one closed compartment, which revealed several guns. He selected a black-plated Glock.

The sights of the guns made her nervous. "Wow, it looks like you're prepared for a war."

"No, but in my new line of work, I never know what I'll be called upon to do. And don't worry since I have a license for all of them."

"I would suspect that you do."

After pulling onto the street, she attempted to look

back at the crime scene. "I hope they can determine who that was that tried to grab me." She covered her face with her hands, rubbing them slightly. *Now, maybe someone will finally believe me.*

"This might be as good a time as ever to talk." His smooth sounding voice relaxed her. "I feel like you know much more than you're telling me."

She knew she had his interest, and that he would be offering his services to her soon. "Like I said, I have a lot of suspicions. I think someone wants me to step down from my judgeship."

"Tell me more about these threats, and why you think so."

"Does that mean you'll help me?" She knew she was pushing, but she needed him.

"It means that I'm curious. I don't like having a shotgun leveled at me either." He accelerated down the street. They wouldn't have long to talk before they reached the station.

"I was hoping to do this quietly, but this attempt on my life has changed all of that. Tell me you'll help me first, and then I'll tell you what I can."

"I might, but on one condition."

"Which is?"

He quickly turned, and focused his haunting, deep-gray eyes on her for a second as he came to a stop. "Help me clear my name. You did mention you had information that I was framed."

"I said that you may have been."

"Have you reported your threats to the police?" He asked, as he avoided a car pulling out in front of them.

"Naturally I have turned over what I could. Many of the threats are so well conceived, or are so subtle, that there's nothing to offer as proof. That is . . . until today."

"I think we'll know very soon who this guy I shot is. They should be running his ID through the computers now." Vance pulled into the parking lot at the police station. "Tell them you came to me concerning adding security to your house. I do that also."

"I live in a guarded community with a guard house."

"I see. You've moved up in the world. Still, I can look at what you have." He turned off the motor. "All should be safe now, but let me come around and get you."

Minutes later, she walked into the front of the police station, where she was met by an officer. "Judge, the police commissioner wants to meet with you personally. He's this way." He turned to Vance. "Another officer will meet with you to take your statement. Please have a seat and check in your weapon while you're here."

Noella started to object to being separated, but changed her mind. "Vance, please stay when you finish. I have more we need to discuss."

"Will do." Vance walked over to the chairs next to the wall, as she watched the officer frown at him. Exactly what was being said about him around the station was not too much of a question since he had made many enemies in his testimony to try to save his neck.

### 

Vance watched Noella disappear around the corner in a very apparent effort to separate them. He prepared to wait. They would get what they could from her first. He had no doubt that he was framed earlier. So, what did Noella know that he had not discovered?

An hour later an officer approached him. "Come on back."

Instead of affording him a comfortable room to discuss the shooting, they ushered him into a room used to question suspects. Surely they were not going to try to pin anything on him this time. He had a circuit judge with him who was being attacked. So much for being the hero of the day.

Detective Garrison walked in behind him. "Hello, Vance. I'm not surprised to see you in here. People seem to die around you."

Vance tightened his fist as he attempted to control his anger. "I think we both know that I didn't ask to be shot at, Garrison."

"What is your connection with the Judge?"

"You have to ask her on that."

"Don't be cute with me. I don't have time for it." Garrison scooted into the seat across from him.

Vance leaned even closer to him. "Watch it, I'm a private citizen now—remember?"

"Yeah, and still leaving a trail of dead people."

Garrison tossed a file in front of him. "Do you recognize any of these people?"

Vance studied the photos. None of them registered. "Should I?"

"These are the two we found in a car not far from where the judge was attacked." He tapped on the photos. "Both of these are from a Mexican cartel that is relocating here. While we have been advised they were here, this is the first confirmation that we have."

"So, you apprehended them?"

"No, we found them like this. Both had been shot by what appears to be a shotgun blast. We'll know soon, but perhaps they have your handiwork in them as well."

"Then this was drug related."

Garrison attempted to avoid the question, but relented. "Maybe yes—maybe no. While we know that they were hit men, exactly who hired them isn't clear."

"What about the guy I shot who was grabbing the judge?"

"There was no identification on him, and that forty-five bullet of yours left a mess out of his face. It will take a while longer to identify him." Garrison glanced over his shoulder. "I know you've established the fact you don't like the people in this station. However, I don't think anyone here set you up, so you can drop the act."

"Why are you so sure?" No! He knew he would never *drop it*.

"I've worked here for over twenty years. I know these people."

"All of them?"

"Most."

"I'm looking for the ones you don't know." He felt no need to back off now, and he knew that making people mad is sometimes the best way to get at the truth.

"You're never going to drop this, are you?"

"If you were in my spot, would you?"

Garrison appeared to be biting his lips, as he contemplated what he would say. "I guess not. All I know for now is that the judge appears to be under some serious threats."

"No shit."

"I have one major problem. She trusts you for some reason, and has asked us to provide you with all the information we have. She wants you to act as her personal bodyguard."

"We both know that she's one of the reasons I'm no longer on the force."

Garrison shook his head. "Yes—life's strange, isn't it. I have been ordered to give you access to anything that might help." He glanced behind him briefly before he moved closer to Vance. "Don't get cocky. You know I'm about as friendly as you'll find here, so don't push it. You made several enemies when you left." He lowered his voice. "You don't think we really have cops on the take in the department, do you?"

Vance could not decide if he could trust Garrison, or not. He decided to hold judgment until later. "Someone set me up and framed me, and I still don't know why. It had to be something I was working on, and something, or someone that I was getting close to uncovering the truth on."

"I'll assure you every case you worked on has been examined by internal affairs."

Vance offered a dull stare, as if he disbelieved him.

Garrison shook his head, apparently knowing he would never win this argument. "You know you're clear to go. I hope you can do us, at least, one favor. We want you to work with a sketcher to give us a composite of the guy you shot."

"I can do that. What about my gun?"

"It will be returned to you shortly. How in the hell are you able to hit anything with a snub-nosed 45?"

Vance decided to hide his hours of practice. "Let's call it blind luck."

"I do want a full report of anything you find while protecting the judge."

"I haven't said I'd take the case yet." Vance pointed to the photos. "Can I have a copy of these?"

"You know, and I know that this meeting never happened." Garrison ignored the photos as if they didn't exist, leaving them for him to have. "Let me know when you would like a friend in the department."

"Sure, but I do need to take the judge back to her car."

"She's already left. Don't worry since she had a full escort." Garrison stood to leave. "Also, take the side door to your truck and keep a low profile. The press is swarming outside the building."

## Chapter 3

Noella turned on the security alarm system as she entered and locked the door to her house. The Baylife Community prided itself on providing the best in security for its residents—the main reason she had purchased a residence there. Still, she knew receiving a special security detail from the state would help. While the house was way too much for one person, she knew it would be a good investment one day after the housing market turned around.

Would Vance call her? Would he keep quiet about her suspicions? Hit men. Why were they after her? Too many questions. She walked to her small office, and saw the messages button blinking on her home phone. She could only imagine how many people would be calling her, but this line was private and given to only her closest friends, or people connected with the court that knew to keep it so.

She activated the playback to a list of four calls in the cue. She slowly listened to another threat, which was very similar to ones she had heard earlier from a guy with a Latin, perhaps Colombian accent. "Hope you got the message this time. We not miss the next time." The caller ID flashed—caller unknown. Since they couldn't trace the previous one, she knew they wouldn't be able to this time either. The other messages had been sent to her office. Now, apparently, they had her private number, and perhaps—her address! A chill quickly spread across her spine as she glanced around the room.

She didn't own a gun—wouldn't know how to fire the damn thing if she did. Thoughts of having to search her entire house overwhelmed her, but where could she go? Anywhere but here.

She grabbed her purse and headed back to her BMW parked in the garage. After finding her cell phone in her purse, she located Vance's number, which he had entered into it, and connected. He answered on the first ring, as her hands continued to shake. "Vance, it's me. I received another threatening call. I don't think I'm alone. Please, help me!"

"Listen to me. If you have a security system, set it off now and it will bring the police. I'm on my way."

###

After he lost connection, Vance tried her number several more times. No answer. Had she set off the alarm? He needed to know.

He called 911. "Listen. I just received a distress call from Judge Peterson, and I'm not sure if she's okay, or not. I can't reach her on the phone now. She lives somewhere in Safety Harbor."

"Who is this?"

"This is Vance Mills. I was just hired by her to provide security."

"We've already received a call from her security company, and the police are on the way."

"Thanks, I am also."

Vance would love to race over the bridge to Safety Harbor, but he knew to be careful. Catching him speeding would be exactly what the police force needed in order to derail his business. While he had very few friends there now, he had to push it. Using her cell phone number, he located her address, and plugged it into his GPS. He had twenty minutes remaining on ETA.

Someone must have known that he was being

delayed at the police department, and therefore leaving her unprotected. While he continued trying to reach her on her cell, his anxiety grew. Why didn't she answer?

After reaching the guard house to her community, he saw a pair of police cars with their blue lights flashing. Good. They were locking down the area.

As an officer approached him, he jumped from his truck and flashed his PI identification. "I'm Vance Mills, and I was just hired by Judge Peterson to provide security."

The officer studied the identification before responding. "She had an intruder, but we think he fled on foot. Someone is with her now."

"Good. I lost connection with her on her phone."

"I need to clear this before you can go through." The officer talked into a microphone clipped to his shoulder. "I have a private detective at the gate who says he was hired by the judge."

Vance waited, as he studied the security house.

"Okay, you're clear. If you can stay with her, it will free up a man to use in finding this guy. We have dogs on the way also."

"I plan to be with her until this over. Let me know if I can do anything else also."

The officer glanced at him. "Are you the guy who shot the two guys earlier?"

Vance blinked. He had another shooting to live with and explain to everyone. "Yeah, it's been a very busy day."

"Do you have any idea what's going on here, or who we're dealing with?"

"Not yet, but I intend to find out."

The officer handed him a card. "If you need to contact me directly, let me know. I'll give you any support I can."

After accepting the card, Vance smiled, as he realized that there were still many good cops doing their job. He needed to decide which ones were, and which ones were not. However, he felt like, just maybe, he could trust this one.

Vance quickly followed the GPS commands through the winding subdivision. The houses looked huge. After finding her house surrounded with police cars, he pulled to one side of the driveway, which was large enough to park ten cars easily. Just how much does a judge make? He also wondered how much her dad was helping her. After quickly reflecting on the past, he remembered how wealthy her dad was, and just like his dad had been until he died.

After rushing to the front door, he was met by another officer. "The judge is waiting for you inside. Do not touch anything since we're still searching for fingerprints."

"Understood. How is she?"

"She's shaking, so try to keep her calm."

While the outside of the house looked impressive enough, the inside exceeded his wildest imagination. Gallery sized paintings hung from the walls. Vases towering above his head decorated the interior rooms. He tried not to look stunned, as he walked on Prussian rugs leaving only a slight view of the oak flooring around the edges.

He soon found her in a small office where she was resting on a sofa. She had a drink in her hand, which she immediately placed on a table when she recognized him.

"I've been trying to call you." He walked closer, as he tried to decide if he should offer her a hug to calm her.

"I'm sorry. I dropped the phone when the alarm went off."

"I had hoped you would set it off."

"I didn't trigger it. It activated on its own."

The tension in his neck tightened. "Did you see who the intruder was?"

"No, I dropped my phone and hid in a closet until the police arrived." Noella pointed to a small storage closet in the office.

"Good for you." Vance motioned to the officers outside. "You're going to be fine now, but let me see what I can find out from the officers."

"Hold on. I'm going with you."

Vance started to resist, but he knew she wanted to know what was going on. "Okay."

Vance followed Noella to a large kitchen, which looked more like a commercial operation. While the stainless steel appliances looked impressive, it was the massive marble topped workstation in the center of the room that was awesome. However, instead of being used for cooking, it now had police equipment on top of it.

Vance smiled at the two officers there. "So . . . what do we have?"

One pointed to a side door leading out to a pool area. Shattered glass covered the floor. Noella raised her hands to her face. "I never heard the glass crash. That must have been what set off the alarm."

"The alarm system does confirm that much. What we're trying to determine is what he used to break it, and if he entered the house."

Without walking on the glass, Vance ventured closer to the door where he saw a small section of the glass with a round hole in it. "That might help." He pointed to it for the officer.

"Definitely."

Noella moved closer. "Why? What is it?"

"I suspect a bullet hole." Vance turned away from the door and scanned the kitchen. If so, the bullet had to lodge somewhere.

Five minutes later, Vance found it hidden in a side panel to a cabinet. The crime scene officer motioned for him to move out of the way. "It's important for us to retrieve the bullet in as much intact shape as we can to be able to match the bullet later with the weapon that fired it."

Vance studied the hole, and then glanced over his shoulder at the center of the glass the bullet came from. Next he studied the angle the glass exploded from the glass which would account for a slight deviation. This angle would give him a nice idea of where the bullet came from.

Vance focused on the policeman. "Has anyone walked the area around the back of the house?"

"Only enough to secure the area. We'll look for additional signs when it gets lighter in the morning."

Vance turned to Noella. "Are you sure you didn't hear a gunshot?"

"No, I only heard the sound of the alarms going off."

Vance readdressed the officers. "Has anyone reported the sound of a gunshot?"

"No, and in this neighborhood where they're so sensitive about security, it would have been reported."

Vance decided to keep his thoughts to himself. Since Noella was not in the room she would not be a target for assassination, but of an attempt to scare her. Since she heard no shot, it either had to be a silencer, or a rifle fired from a long distance off. Both cases suggested they wanted to frighten her, and not kill her.

The officer went to a large window and peeked out past a curtain. "This area has many wooded areas where someone can hide. We'll maintain the perimeters until morning, and then fully check it out. A helicopter will be here in a minute with infrared sensors. If he's in there we'll see him."

"Until you do, we need to take her somewhere she can be safe."

Noella spoke up. "I'm not going to be run out of my home. As of right now, I have an army of police around. This will be the safest place for me."

The officer glanced at Vance. "She might be right, but that's your call."

"I'll need to cancel my hearings in the court tomorrow. Luckily, it's a very slow day. My legal assistant can do this, and I'll call her shortly." She pulled her business suit closer around her neck. "I'm not too sure I can sleep tonight, and I do want to be here when they check the outside of the house, and the woods around here tomorrow morning."

Vance knew that he had little choice but to help

also. "I wasn't prepared for this, but you do need all the protection you can receive tonight. I'll need a couch."

"A couch?"

"Well, it's up to you." He hoped that she would realize they needed to talk more about what was going on, and that this would be the best way to do it.

"Okay. Agreed." She turned to the officer. "Is it okay if I start a pot of coffee? I think it will be a while before any of us gets any sleep tonight."

## Chapter 4

Finally, the last of the intruders inside her house had left, and the back door had been sealed with a piece of plywood. Her insurance agent had promised an early morning replacement. To hell with the coffee—where was that new bottle of tequila?

After walking to the side table in the dining room, she opened a door to her hidden liquor stash. She hardly considered herself an alcoholic, but a bottle of wine late at night was always nice, especially if she had guests over. The tequila, well that was something she learned to enjoy in Mexico.

She turned towards Vance. "Care to join me?"

"When did you take up drinking tequila?"

"It's a habit I learned in Mexico. Going on a cruise to Cancun has been one of my best ways to get away and relax. I work most of the time when I'm here."

"I see. Still the same, I think I need to stay awake, and alert tonight."

In case he changed his mind later, Noella placed two glasses on the table top before she quickly strolled to the kitchen to find a couple of limes. She really needed to get out of her business suit, and into something more comfortable. How much more comfortable remained a question. Whatever. She had several full length robes she could use to cover up with.

"I often drink it the traditional way that they do in Mexico, but tonight I think a margarita would be nice. Do you know how to make them?"

She watched him smile at the simple challenge. "I think I can manage. Frozen, or over the rocks?"

"Rocks will be fine. I'll be back in a minute. This suit has to come off." Noella turned, and left him to it. This would give her a few minutes to collect her thoughts. She needed to think, and to decide how much to tell him.

After walking into her bedroom, which was the coldest room in the house, she realized that she never spent any time in there except to sleep. While her giant, king-sized bed definitely had enough room to romp all night, she, however, always slipped into a corner at the top, and to the left. It made refreshing the covers in the mornings easier.

While removing her clothes after closing the door, she felt slightly apprehensive. While she felt like she could trust Vance, he was still a strange man in her house. She quickly slipped into a nightshirt, keenly aware that she had no panties on now. She reached for a robe. After glancing at her hair in the mirror, she stopped at her dressing area inside her walk-in closet, and reached for a brush. Why did she feel like she had to prep for Vance? She knew she would be going to bed as soon as the drink hit her, and they talked briefly.

When she walked back to the dining room where he was waiting for her, she watched him relaxing in a chair with his back to her. She took the moment to study his wide broad shoulders under the crisp clean blue shirt that he wore. He had always entranced her with his physique, and his charisma that he thought he didn't have, but which she knew better. His long, black hair had a healthy shine reflecting a life style that she knew he maintained. Memories of running her fingers through his locks returned.

She couldn't stand there too much longer, or he would know she was fantasizing about him. That would be a message she really didn't want to send right now. She walked in front of him and stopped. "How about that drink?"

Vance pointed to the table. "I think you might like it. You didn't have exactly what I needed, so I had to improvise some."

"I didn't think you drank, so how did you learn to make them?" Curiosity made her fill in the missing pieces while she waited for him to answer. She remembered his dad dying, and about how he had to leave law school to find a job. With his world crashing in on him then, she would have loved to help him, but he wouldn't allow it. In fact, the opposite happened, and he refused to see her again.

"I'm not opposed to drinking socially, but have other uses for my time and money." He reached over and offered her the drink.

Noella accepted the drink, and slowly analyzed the taste. "Hummm . . . okay, how did you make it taste so good?"

"Trade secret." He soon relented, and pointed to a

mix in the bottom of the cabinet.

"Humm, I don't remember buying that."

"Before you have too much to drink, I think we need to talk for a minute. We might not have a lot of privacy tomorrow."

"Agreed. I know you have questions, and there are some things you need to know to help you and me."

"I'm listening."

"First, let me tell you what I do know before I mention what I suspect. I expect all of this to stay confidential." She waited for him to nod an approval. "A month ago I started getting calls, which included the typical hang up when I answered. These came to my cell and the office. They only came when I first arrived at the office, or drove in the car. I took it as a sign they knew where I was all of the time."

"You said that you had the police look into this, as well as the phone companies?"

"Naturally. No records of the calls existed."

"In other words, the police don't believe your story."

"Exactly. However, I think that all changed today." Noella glanced at her smashed out glass door.

"I know you had a conversation with the police commissioner today."

"Yes, and we'll have a bigger conversation tomorrow. Unless I can prove these attacks are on me as a judge, I'll receive no state or local protection other than what any other citizen would receive. He wanted me to prove this was related to my work. Now . . . how am I supposed to do that?"

Vance quietly considered her comments while he made plans. "While you're talking to the commissioner tomorrow, I need to find out more about who your attackers might be. I heard it could be hit men from Mexico, but for some reason, I suspect they came from Miami. Listen, I know you have a lot of information that you cannot give me, but if you want me to help I need to know a few things."

"Such as?

"For a short list, let's start with the cases you're working on now. Since you feel someone is asking you to step down there must be a reason, or a connection. I need to know everything on your docket, and what could be coming on it in the very near future."

"Most of this information is public knowledge. I have an assistant who can help you with it tomorrow."

"I know you have your suspicions, and have thought about it. Are any of your trials rising to the top that I need to look at first?"

She closed her eyes for a second and shook her head. "Nothing that really stands out, and trust me I've done some serious thinking about this."

Vance nodded his head, as if he understood. "Listen. I'm sure you have. Have the police offered any suggestions on who this might be?"

"I hear a lot of cases on drugs and gangs. These would be the only people I can think of that would have motive, and the resources to cause me any problems." She thought of any back room deals that defense lawyers, and the prosecution had tried to work out with her, and which ones might have made someone mad.

"I see. You mentioned that you think someone wants you to step down. This is different from forcing you to rule a certain way. Why do you think such?"

"I've never received a message telling me to step down, but it's the way the police talk to me. You know. It's the little comments like 'you should expect such in this line of work, and if you can't take the heat maybe you need to do something else besides being a judge'."

"That sounds like the group of hyenas that sold me out."

Noella felt the internal analysis going on inside Vance's head, as he appeared to be putting the pieces together. He was close, and she needed to be careful what she told him. Call it a hunch, one she needed his help on, but the people wanting her to step down, and the ones who turned on Vance earlier, were the same officers. Was this a coincidence, or brutal facts?

Noella waited for Vance, who was taking his time, and apparently choosing his words carefully. "You know I'll need the names of those you talked to that have advised you to step down."

"I thought you might, but you know that you can say nothing about my suspicions. You know that these are the same guys who also pushed for your expulsion."

"You mentioned we would have some common interest. I think I know how to be discrete, and without you saying a word about which officers in internal affairs you're talking about."

"I think you see my problem, and why I wanted someone outside to help me."

"Yes. If the attempt on your life today had not happened we might have had an element of surprise. It definitely appears they don't want you talking to me." Vance paused for a minute to massage his eyes. "If you suspect internal affairs of being behind this, why haven't you talked to the mayor or the feds on this?"

"I have talked to the mayor and the state bureau also. Both said I needed proof, but assured me that they will conduct their own evaluation. I'm not sure how much support I'll get from them without a formal complaint." Noella finished the rest of her drink. "Not bad. Can I have another?"

He smiled as he relaxed his intense expressions of concern and intrigue. "It's your booze and your house." He walked over to the liquor cabinet and retrieved the tequila.

As Vance worked on the drink, she pondered the real question she had. What was behind all of this? Why was she considered to be such a threat? And to whom?

Vance handed her the drink. "You know if I get you drunk enough, you'll tell me everything."

"I doubt if that will happen. I also doubt if you're the kind of guy who would ever take advantage of a girl in distress." She knew many guys would, but not him. On the few dates she had allowed herself to try, the guys all had one intention it seemed—apply liquor, and try to get in her pants. Some were much more subtle than others, but all wanted the same end result—her bedroom.

"You never know. We had a history once, and I've been told to never say never." As his focus penetrated her thoughts, the grayish color of his eyes managed to hide his true intentions, making him the one person she could never read. She had never understood the real reason why he left her, and perhaps she never would. They had shared an intense relationship, and great sex. She always assumed that they were almost to that point of marriage.

If only his dad had not died. She shook her head to clear the memories. That was then, and now is now. "I remember telling you those words long ago."

Vance leaned closer. "Don't worry. Some secrets are meant to be exactly that. You've done well for yourself and I've always been proud of you."

As Noella started to speak, he seemed to understand where she was going and lifted a finger to her lips to delay words that needed to be avoided for now. "We need to concentrate on the problem at hand. Then we might talk—deal?"

Noella breathed easier. "You're right. However, I've always had many unanswered question from back then that I wanted answers to. But I do respect your privacy, and wishes." The slight touch of his finger to her lips had felt like a lightning rod passing energy between them. She felt it. Did he?

If he did, he hid his emotions extremely well. "There are several things that we need to work on. Why do they want you to step down versus rule a certain way? Why would another judge rule differently?" He offered a sly smile. "You haven't made a reputation as a *hanging judge,* have you?"

While slightly offended, she returned the smile before she replied, "I think I've used professional judgment on all of my sentences. If not, they can always appeal, and on any major case that is to be expected."

"I understand, but to make this easier, can you, at least, tell me which cases you're currently handling that involve someone with the means and determination to hire a hit man. You must have really pissed off someone in the past, or they believe you'll rule against them on an upcoming case."

"I keep wondering about which case it would have to be. I keep going over any ongoing or upcoming case which has already been assigned to me." Noella enjoyed more of the margarita. "Trust me I have been over and over this list. I don't understand how I would decide any case differently from any other judge. The thought has occurred to me that they might try to threaten me into ruling a certain way. But no attempt to contact me on such has been made yet."

"Tomorrow morning they should have an ID on the guy I shot, and more information on the others found dead. I'll do my best to try to make some connections." He rubbed his chin, apparently studying his need for a shave. "It'll be interesting to see how much cooperation I receive from the police department."

"With that, I can help. If you have any problems at all, call me. The police commissioner knows I won't tolerate any problems, and he also knows that I'm close to having the state bureau look into this."

She watched Vance glance around. "I know we have people outside, so all I need to do in here is just relax until tomorrow morning. However, I know you need to get some sleep."

"Yes, I do. This drink helps. Thank you." She stood, and pointed down a hallway. "I have an extra bedroom you can use."

"I appreciate the offer, but I think a couch in the center of the house will be better. I can sleep later."

"Suit yourself. You can watch TV if you wish, and especially if you can keep the sound down. There's also a small blanket on the side if you get cold during the night."

"Thanks. I'll be fine."

The drinks clouded her thoughts. How strong did he make them? The mix he used must have hid their potency, as she stumbled slightly into his arms. The strength and stability in them rushed back so many memories. While their affair was short lived, the memories and fantasies had only intensified over the years.

While she had made it fine on her own for a long time, this silent moment stretched into a minute. She could not deny the need she had for someone to hold her close. Considering she had been almost kidnapped on the street by a hired hit man, she thought she had held up fine. Nothing would be wrong in enjoying a little comfort from a man in her past.

He appeared to understand. But . . . no, she needed to go to bed quickly, and before she slipped further into a mistake that she would have a hard time correcting later. She straightened her back and pulled away. "Thank you. This has been a very trying day for me."

"Here. Let me help you to the bedroom."

Alarms went off. No. This was too personal, and too much of a temptation. *Why did he have to look so damn good?* "It's okay. I can make it. Thank you for staying with me tonight."

Before she could back away, he leaned over and offered her a kiss on her forehead, which was much like he had in the past. With his six foot height compared to her five foot and two inches, it made for an easy connection. "I'm sure you'll feel better tomorrow." Vance paused, as he pointed toward her office. "One last thing. Do you mind if I use your computer to connect to the internet and do some research?"

At first she felt apprehensive, but soon agreed as she was really too tired to care. She slowly realized that he might need it in order to help her. "Sure. Let me set it up for you."

Seconds later, she escorted him to her small office, and the library where she spent a lot of her time. "As they say, knock yourself out since I'm going to bed."

"Thanks. This will keep me busy for a while."

She turned and walked to her bedroom. Enough. She wanted to sleep, but could she? While her body wanted to rest, her mind raced. She pulled the covers to one side, and slipped inside the comfort of her bed.

###

Vance waited for her to turn out the lights before he searched for what he wanted to know. What cases were on her docket? He also wanted to see what major arrest had occurred in the last few months that would be working their way to her? He needed to find all possible cases that she would be involved with. While this is something he would check again with her assistant, he wanted to leave nothing to chance.

After completing his list, he knew the hardest part to obtain would be the cases being reviewed by internal affairs. They always maintained a veil of secrecy that even extended to the elite in the force. For this, he would need an insider, something he had trouble with when he tried to clear his name the first time. However, this time he had a new card to play— the chief of police, and the mayor had agreed to give him unlimited access. While this cooperation remained to be seen, he planned to use any resources he had while he had the chance.

Previous cases she had ruled on shouldn't be reason enough to have her step down, that is, unless revenge was involved. Since this was not fully out of the realm of things, he added a few more cases that he needed to investigate. An hour later, he realized exactly how much of a load she handled. No wonder she acted tired, and loved to go to Cancun to get away.

Finishing some of his research, he considered one more scenario. She was not elected, but had to run for her judgeship. Who were the opponents she ran against, and did anyone have any grudges against her that he needed to investigate? After another hour of work, he hit a dead end. She had won easily with not much opposition. He dad had helped her, and had provided the money for her to run a successful campaign.

Somehow he realized he was missing something. He scratched his head, and glanced at his watch. He needed to catch a few hours of sleep if he was going to be worth anything later today. He closed the computer and headed for the couch. Why hadn't he taken her up on the vacant bed offer?

###

Noella had twisted and turned all night. How could it be time to get out of bed? However, she knew the police would be back early in the morning to complete their work. Had they located the intruder in the woods? Nevertheless, she needed to shower and get prepared for the day. While she had planned on rescheduling her docket for today, she still intended on making an appearance later.

First, she needed to check on Vance. She hadn't heard any noises, but assumed he was still in the house. She stood and reached for her robe, pulling it tightly around her. Knowing her long hair would be a mess, she stopped by her dressing room, and reached for her brush. Call it vanity, but she often wished she could spend more time on her looks. The excessive time she spent working, and the lack of a real boyfriend, had molded her into who she was—a judge.

As she started to tip toe out of her room, she started to hunt for him. He wasn't in the kitchen, which had a light on. The plywood boarded door ushered back memories of the night before. Would she really be safe here, and especially after Vance went on his merry way?

While a small light was on in her office, the computer had been turned off. Exactly what he was looking for would be interesting to know, and if he had found it. She thought about checking her own e-mail, but hesitated since she needed to find Vance first. Should she call his name?

Quietly, she proceeded to another room she enjoyed, which was a sunroom facing the backyard pool. She saw him there, as she edged around a large pot holding flowers, and plants extending to the twelve foot ceiling.

He had found a mat to use while exercising, or what appeared to be yoga of some kind. Entranced, she paused to watch him. He had his weight on one leg, and his hands together in a sort of prayer offering. His right foot rested firmly against his left knee.

After a two or three minute period, he slowly lowered his foot, and turned toward her. "I thought you might be getting up soon."

Okay. So he knew she was watching him. "Yes. I needed to start getting ready, and I was wondering what you were doing. What was that you were doing?"

"It's some simple morning exercises that I have created from learning many disciplines. It helps to keep me sharp and ready for another day. I'm sure the police will be here early, so you do need to hurry. They may want to search the entire house again for any evidence of him actually coming inside."

"Well, I'm going to take a shower, so be sure to

keep them out of my area."

"Will do." As Vance walked closer to her, he looked like he could also use a shower, as he apparently had worked up a nice sweat while doing his exercise. While the stubble on his face added to his masculine allure, the hardest temptation she had to deal with was his scent—so intoxicating, yet something she had to ignore.

"Vance, I'm not big into cooking, but you're welcome to see if you can find anything to eat in the kitchen."

Vance glanced toward the kitchen. "Thanks. I'll see what I can do."

"Did you get any sleep last night?"

"Yes . . . some, but I'll take a nap later. It appears I've turned into a night person. That is when I do a lot of my work these days."

After glancing at him, she could only imagine. "I guess I can understand that. I'll be back in a little bit." She turned to leave, but would have loved to stay and talk. Having someone inside her house was different. Until now, she had never considered herself lonely.

After walking into her bedroom, she stopped and

locked the door. It wasn't that she mistrusted Vance, it was the thoughts of the police walking in on her that made her want to hurry. Being a judge ushered in a whole new era of responsibilities on her. She couldn't have a girl's night out partying, or a relationship that could be twisted into a scandal. While she won the last election easily, the next time it might not be such. She had to be ready to defend her work, and her reputation.

She removed her robe, and hung it on its spot. Since her night dress needed to be washed, she dropped it in the hamper. The sense of being totally naked had never crossed her mind in the mornings, but today, she had a man in her house.

After stepping into the shower, she soon felt the instant gratification of the hot water. Even the body wash she used to caress her body offered her new sensations. It had been a long time since she had a boyfriend of any kind. The last time was a guy she met on one of her cruises. It was a dumb mistake, as far as flings went, but a mistake was better than nothing.

As usual, she soon stayed too long in the shower, and she now needed to hurry. She wanted to look like a professional when the police arrived, which meant wearing full make up, and being dressed appropriately. At least for a while, she knew she needed Vance to provide constant protection for her. What if he had other clients? Could he be at her total disposal? She had never asked. Bad of her, but she would ask in a few minutes if he could provide the around the clock protection she needed.

She sniffed the air. Was that food she smelled? Damn, it was overwhelming. She had to hurry.

### 

Vance used what he could, but Noella wasn't wrong about cooking—ever. It must be nice to go out to eat all of the time. Still, he found a bag of flour he used for biscuits, and made some milk gravy to add to them. He hoped she was okay with him unthawing a small steak to add to it. The last three eggs she had in the refrigerator would have to be split between them.

While he had glanced out the windows several times to make sure no one was around, he felt sure the intruder had disappeared long ago. Everything he wanted would be in the report.

As soon as he finished, he heard the door opening from her bedroom. She approached him as fresh as ever, and leaving him to squirm slightly as he rubbed his scrubby face. Oh yeah, he probably smelled some also.

They needed to discuss their plans for the next few days. While he had some investigative work he needed to take care of, it was nothing that he couldn't push to a later date. As a side note, the money from this new case would be good. He hoped she realized that his services wouldn't be free, and she obviously had the funds to pay him. Still, it needed to be discussed.

When she walked closer, his mind forgot about business, and centered on her as a woman. Despite the business suit she had on now, he recognized the body underneath. Her breasts were firm and large for her height and weight. Apparently, she had changed very little since they were a couple.

He placed the eggs next to the steak and biscuits before moving the plate to the counter top where the chairs had been arranged to enjoy this in-kitchen dining. He pointed to the gravy. "I know this is not a very healthy meal, but it's what I could find."

She smiled as she looked over the small feast. "I

never eat this much in the morning. However, it smells fantastic. I didn't know you could cook like this."

"This is nothing. You know they say breakfast is your most important meal."

"I understand, but this is a lot of trouble for one person. In my case I can't run late for work."

"Since you mentioned it, how do you really like being a judge?" He had not planned on asking this, but he had wondered why she wanted to sit on the bench. She could be making much more in private practice with her dad.

"It's what I wanted to do most of my life. The hardest part was first working the five years as a lawyer, which is required to hold office. Winning the race was fantastic."

"For what it's worth, I voted for you." The truth was he had followed her career very closely. However, seeing her in her big, beautiful house only confirmed why he had not seen her since law school. They now lived in totally different worlds. His dad had money once, but when he died they discovered he also had major debts. This left his mother with no choice but to file for bankruptcy on his estate, and hunt for a job.

She had never worked before.

"I appreciate your vote for sure." He watched her take her seat, and taste the food. "Hey, with a guy like you around I would lose my *girly* figure in no time."

Vance decided to walk into the discussion she had opened. "I guess we need to discuss exactly what you want to hire me to do."

"Obviously, I want you to pursue an investigation into what is going on. I want to know who is behind these attacks and why. I'm sure you also understand I need a personal bodyguard until this is over."

"Around the clock coverage will include me hiring additional help."

"I understand, but I want you to handle all personal travel and appearances that I make. I think that while I'm in the courthouse I'll be safe enough. It's only when I leave there."

"I agree. It's later at night when we need to have someone posted outside your house."

"I was thinking about that, and wondering. Now, I don't want you to get the wrong message, but I was thinking about asking you to stay with me until this is over."

The request surprised him. A scandal could definitely climb out of this. "Around the clock protection is not cheap."

"I think I can get the court to cover some of this cost, but you know I have the funds, or I can get them from my dad."

This confirmed that her dad was still giving her support. Interestingly, where was her father with all of this going on?

He started to ask, but she interrupted his thoughts. "My dad isn't happy about me leaving his firm. He sees no future in being a judge. He has been very successful in his practice, and wants me to be a partner there one day."

"Do you think you'll ever go back into private practice?"

"Perhaps one day, but it's not my passion."

Discussing exactly why she wanted to be a judge would be interesting, but he knew he would have lots of time to do this over the next few days. "I'm not sure how long this will take to get answers. If this is alright with you, let's work on this a week at a time."

"Perfect. Then you'll take care of me?"

"Yes, but I think we need to keep the fact I'm staying here a secret. The privacy afforded by this community will help." Vance watched her finish the breakfast before he continued, "I think we need to do some shopping for food." Before she could answer, Vance heard a knock on the door. "I'll get it while you finish your coffee. I'm sure it will be the police. I want to check outside with them now that we have some light to work with."

In truth, he wanted to hear what they knew without Noella close to him. Since part of his job would be to keep her calm, he knew that he could do that much better by dealing with everything discretely.

As he closed the door behind him, he saw two uniformed officers waiting for him outside. "She had a rough night, but she is getting ready to go to the courthouse."

"We understand. We wanted her to know we were outside, and we needed to see if we can find anything behind the house."

"I've been waiting on you also. I want to go with you."

"Understood, but remember we're treating this as

a crime scene, and you'll need to follow our lead."

"Understood. I assume no one saw anything last night from the helicopter, or from the perimeter?"

"Nothing. It was a long night. We also turned some dogs loose, and found nothing. The shot could have come from anywhere."

He already suspected it was a rifle that could have been a long way off. He had used Google map last night to analyze the area. Her house had too much exposure. Before tonight, he had to make some adjustments.

Without another word they walked around the outside of the house. The number of doors and windows made this place a nightmare to cover.

One officer decided to make conversation. "You would think in a neighborhood like this you would not have to worry about being shot at."

"Yeah, well someone did."

"The homeowner association is not happy. They've ordered additional security until we get to the bottom of this."

"That's good to know. The judge also has hired me to provide twenty-four hour bodyguard service for her."

The two officers nodded at each other. "Let us know what we can do to help. We all like the judge."

"I may need to hire some additional men. If I do, I'll have them register with the guard." Vance knew word of him staying there would circulate if he didn't make advanced plans to hide it.

### 

Noella waited for them to finish their search around the house. Before they did, she heard the door bell ring. She glanced out the peep hole, and saw a man carrying a large window pane. *Good, that needed to be replaced.*

However, waiting on the repair might make her late getting to the court house. She opened the door and smiled. "Hi, I was hoping you would get here first thing this morning. How long will this take?"

"Maybe thirty minutes. This isn't a hard job."

"Okay, come on in."

After he glanced around, the guy smiled and walked in.

"Here, let me show you where it is." She stopped for a second. "How did you know the exact size of the window?"

"Your insurance agent e-mailed us the specs on the house last night."

Was it that easy to get information on her house? If so, who else could invade another layer of her privacy? "I see."

Vance walked in, and studied the repairman before turning toward Noella. "Getting this in place will be good, but we need to work on tighter security later today."

"I'll leave that up to you. Right now, I need to get to the courthouse to handle a few things. I assume you want to follow me there."

"I think you need to let me drive you. My truck will attract less attention, and the windows are bulletproof."

"Really. Who exactly did you buy this truck from?"

"You don't want to know," he joked. "You know this is one of those *if I tell you I have to shoot you.*"

"Not funny."

Vance shrugged it off. "Sorry, but it's the best way to keep you safe. We need to wait until this guy finishes installing the door. I can reconnect the sensor that was on the previous glass."

Noella gave up her push to hurry. "I'm going to check on my e-mail while we wait."

A few minutes later, she received a call. Her insurance company's name showed on the caller ID. "Hello, I wanted to let you know we're having trouble reaching our window repair guy this morning, but hopefully it will not be much longer."

"Wait, we have a guy here now."

"He's not from us. Did you get a name?"

"No, hold on." She walked to the edge of her office and motioned for Vance. He strolled over.

"Here, take this call." She offered a suspicious glance toward the guy at the window, and hoped Vance would understand.

Vance retrieved the phone, but kept an eye toward the repairman. "This is Vance Mills, and I'm providing security for the judge. What is it?"

"Whoever you have there doing the work wasn't sent by us."

"Understood."

Vance swirled as the repairman suddenly

produced a pistol. With incredible speed, Vance slammed into the guy and knocked him to the floor before he could point it. As they fought over the gun, Noella screamed while running for the front door, and hopefully where the police officers were.

BAM! The gun blast shattered her remaining nerves. The two officers quickly drew their guns as they ran inside. A third officer grabbed her, and pulled her to one side.

"Oh my God, Vance!" Before receiving an answer to her scream, she covered her face with her hands. Was Vance shot? Did the guy still have a gun? The eerie quiet lingered as she waited.

One officer slowly emerged, and yelled into his side microphone that was pinned to his uniform. "I need back up. We have someone here who has been shot. There's been another attempt on the judge's life. We're not sure if the outside is secure. I repeat, we need back up now! We're inside the judge's house."

"Please confirm—you have one person shot?"

"That is correct. We'll hold up in here until backup arrives."

Vance walked out with blood on his t-shirt. She

couldn't control a scream. "You're shot!"

"No, it's not mine." Vance turned to the officer next to Noella. "How did this guy get past the guard at the entrance?"

"I don't know." The officer retrieved his phone and quickly called the guard house. "There's no answer."

The other officer activated his shoulder mic again. "I think we may have another officer down at the guard station. There's no answer."

The sound of sirens in the distance confirmed that every policeman in a fifty mile radius was on the way there now. She studied Vance, and the blood on him. She wanted to grab him, to hold him. He had saved her life again.

### 

Vance stood near one side of Noella's office, as she grilled the men in front of her. The list ran long as sheriff deputies, police captains, a field officer for the FBI no less, all stood at attention, as she demanded answers.

"An individual doesn't get these kinds of threats on their life. It has to be because I'm a judge. These people just didn't blow in here without someone being behind this. I want to know who it is, and I want to know now!"

The FBI agent spoke first. "Since this guy was dead when we arrived, I doubt he'll be telling us anything. We're running a check on him, and have drawn a blank so far. It's highly likely he was brought in from outside the country where we would have no records on him. It's like he was sent on a suicide mission."

"Are we talking about an international crime syndicate of some sort?" Vance asked, as he decided to make his presence known.

"Who knows at this point? You didn't give us a chance to talk to him." The FBI agent glanced at the judge. "I think the most important thing now is to keep you safe. With two attempts here in the last twenty-four hours, I think it's safe to assume they know where you live. We need to see about having someone cover for you at the court for a while."

"No, that's exactly what someone is trying to do—remove me from the chair. It's your job to try to figure out why."

"You know it'll be almost impossible to provide around the clock coverage for you, and especially if you go back and forth to the courthouse."

"I expect you to do your job, and I'll do mine." She glanced at Vance. "I also have a fulltime bodyguard with me."

"Now that this has become a federal matter, I don't think you need a private bodyguard."

"Excuse me. It's only because of him that I'm still alive. Do I make myself clear?"

"He'll have to follow our lead, and coordinate everything with us."

"Wrong! The only person he has to coordinate with is me."

Vance watched Noella handle this guy like he was a kid. She knew her stuff, and he felt glad she was the one talking to the agent like this, and not him. This was the kind of guy who could make life on him unbearable if he wanted to.

The agent shook his head. "Fine, have it your way."

Another uniformed officer walked in. "I hate to bring more bad news, but they found the guard working the front gate. He had been shot in the back of the head."

The room remained quiet for several moments. Vance had suspected this. There had been no reports of gun shots. The attacker must have used the silencer they found in his workbag earlier. I assume this was probably what he had intended to use after he got the chance inside the house. Luckily Vance had prevented the assassin from doing so.

The Sheriff moved forward. "As of right now I have two homicides on my turf, and this house is a crime scene. It'll be a while until I can release it to the judge. She'll have to find somewhere else to live until then."

"No problem. I know where I can stay," Noella informed everyone, "and this time no one will know but me and Vance. While it's too late to go to the courthouse now, I'll be there tomorrow. I expect someone to give me some answers then."

The FBI agent didn't look too happy about the situation. "I think we can provide you better protection than one bodyguard."

"Well so far, he has saved my life like I said *two*

*times,* and until now I never received any assistance, even after asking for it for a while. I think I'll go with Vance. However, I'm sure he could use your help. Any leads you get on this I expect to be given to me and to him for follow up. I hope I make myself clear."

# Chapter 5

Vance quickly loaded her suitcase into the back of his truck. While she had not told him where she had in mind to go to, he knew a few places where they could disappear. Then again, with her *family money,* he assumed they owned many different properties that would be available to her. It would require some fast checking on his part, but anywhere would be better than at her place. Someone was apparently very pissed off at her.

After being escorted by several uniformed officers to Vance's truck, the FBI agent handed him a card. "I need to know where you are. Please call me when you settle in."

Vance accepted the card and casually tossed it into a small compartment. "Everything is up to the judge. I work for her, and right now she trusts no one."

"Still, we'll give you a police escort until you get on the interstate."

"That's fine." Vance expected this. It would give

him time to talk to Noella and see what she had on her mind. He also needed to stop by his place to retrieve some clothes sometime.

Vance walked around the truck and helped Noella into her seat as he studied the guys watching him. Who could he really trust, and who was secretly plotting against her? Something didn't add up.

Minutes later, he hit the gas going over the causeway toward Tampa. "I think I need to ask you where we're going."

"First, we need to lose everyone. I assume you know how to do that."

"Yes, but it'll take some time. I'm sure they have the truck bugged. Don't worry, I can find it when we stop."

"They wouldn't dare."

"They're just doing what they think best." He retrieved the card with the FBI agent's number on it. "Here. Write this number down somewhere for me, and then I'll show you something."

After she scribbled the number and name down on a small pad she had retrieved from her purse, she handed him the card. After tearing it in half, he pointed to a small wire, and a metallic implant. "Yes, they plan to track our every move." He tossed the card back on the dashboard. "We can use this to our advantage in a few minutes.

A hundred miles north on Interstate seventy-five he pulled over, and headed for a gas station. "Stay inside, and I'll take care of everything. Minutes later, he had removed three more bugs. They were good, but he thought he had them all. This was one area he was well trained in. After a quick walk around the parking lot, he had replaced these on various cars. This should give them nightmares. He had to leave before they knew what he did, and thus gain some time.

Vance kind of liked her plan. Her dad owned a boat he hardly ever used. It was maintained to keep the firm's fat-cat clients happy when they came to Florida. She had made a call to her father, telling him that an old friend wanted to use it.

Vance had listened to the call closely. Most dads, he thought, would show more concern. His daughter had been attacked several times the last few hours. Instead, he only wanted to know how she planned to handle the situation, and if she needed any money.

Some dad.

After pulling into a hotel parking lot close to the International Shopping Mall, he soon found a taxi and transferred her luggage to it. He would leave the truck there, hoping that if they find it, they would think he had checked into the hotel with her. Knowing they would find out the truth soon, he needed to move fast and execute one last surprise for them as they disappeared on her dad's boat.

### 

The weather looked fantastic as they entered Clearwater Beach, with the blue skies and crisp clean air reflecting the touristy atmosphere of the small beach community. Noella thought that her dad's boat would be a perfect place for her to hide.

Noella pointed to the front entrance of the new Hyatt. Seconds later, she handed the driver money for the fare. After he passed the luggage to them, a guy wearing a uniform from the hotel quickly rushed to retrieve them. She needed the cab driver to think they were staying there. She felt sure the police, or the FBI would find the cab driver and ask him later.

Inside, she motioned to the hotel staff to leave the

luggage by a chair inside. "We can take it from here. We're not ready to check in yet."

"No problem." He looked surprised, but complied as he walked away.

Moments later they were hurrying across the street toward the marina. After some quick safety checks they would be rushing out to sea, and headed back towards Tampa where they could dock the boat. Noella found the key to the security entrance and handed it to Vance. "This is a big boat. I'll need your help."

"I've been operating boats since I was a kid. This will not be a problem." After he opened the gate, they walked on the boat.

Yes, she knew that when his dad was alive they had money and many friends who probably owned boats. Together they could handle the boat, and with a little luck they could make it to Tampa before it got too dark. She knew a couple of places they could dock it, but she would finalize it with Vance as they got closer.

The fifty-five foot cruiser had all the amenities they would need, including two separate state rooms.

This was not intended to be a romantic cruise. Still, the idea of such one day later in her life would be nice.

She checked the electronics while she prepared to get underway as quickly as possible. Vance was doing an inspection of the outside. After hearing an all clear, she cranked the main engine, allowing it time to warm before they headed out. All they had to do now was disconnect from the land power and cast off.

Noella walked to the door and glanced out. All appeared to be quiet. "Vance, are you ready?"

"All looks good out here. Did you check the gas?"

"Yes, cast us off, and help me navigate the marina. It will be much easier after we get into the channel." Since it was her dad's boat, and she had operated it before, she hoped Vance wouldn't mind her taking the helm.

Vance soon appeared dock side, and waved at her. "All clear."

Seconds later, he walked in next to her. "The marina is tight, watch for my hand signals." He offered her a quick hand pat on her shoulder. More like a big brother, but very welcomed.

Noella glanced at the sun edging closer to the

horizon. It would be late when they arrived in Tampa. Enjoying the sunset would be nice since she needed to relax, and she knew her dad always kept nice wine on board. She felt the relief flow through her, as she throttled away from the dock. This boat should make sure they were totally isolated from the world, and hopefully the danger hunting her.

As tempting as it was to go through the narrows where the water was smoother, she knew to get out to deep water as quickly as possible. After making it around the corner, she turned right and started past the beach clubs, which were swinging into the typical festive mood of the evening. As usual, many boats were docked outside with party people making trips back and forth. This was the place where the beautiful people, the muscle bound studs, and the hot girls hung out. It had been a while, but she remembered the times when she was younger, and not so tied to her career.

Vance reentered the cabin and touched the wheel. "I can take this if you want me to."

"Sure, but be careful until we get out past the breakers." Okay, maybe she was a little protective of her dad's boat. As much as she liked being on the water, she wished she had used it more often. Drinking wine and watching a sunset would be a great way to relieve some of her stress, but still, she really needed a second person on board to handle the boat.

Vance took the wheel, and nodded to his right. "This place never changes. I come here occasionally. I still remember the times we had fun here many years ago."

"Really! I don't think I've ever stopped in here since we quit dating." She had wondered when they would get around to their history. Getting answers to what happen between them would be interesting, but not now—later.

Vance appeared to be biting his lips, as he bid his time. "Don't worry. I know as a judge you have a reputation to protect. My lips are sealed."

"I see. We do have a few secrets to maintain, and I do appreciate it." Yes, they had visited the club across from them several times when they were dating in law school. While she shouldn't allow her thoughts to remember one certain night, she couldn't help it.

"You're welcome." The one thing she had always counted on before was Vance's honor.

However, Noella turned from Vance to hide her face, and the expression she knew that would be registering on her smile. After staying late one night and sneaking to a far side of the beach, they had allowed their passions to get the best of them. Perhaps more than slightly drunk they had made love for the first time. It was also her first time ever.

She had bled. The towel they used had to be hidden after she finally quit bleeding. It had scared her and maybe even him more than her, but calling for a medic was out of the question. Her dad would go ballistic.

How long would it be before someone dug into their past, and put their connections together? She never did anything illegal, or unethical. While he was a material witness in a case she heard, he did so in a professional manner on the police force. In fact, he was never called to the stand. Strange, but the prosecutor must have had a reason.

The exact details had always been hazy, but the most important fact was that an innocent person had been shot—shot by Vance. Yes, he had also shot two top members of a violent crime family. However, she and the police force agreed that his actions were both ruthless and irresponsible.

The case could have become very messy with him actually being charged for manslaughter. The deal worked out was to have him dismissed from the force, or even better have him resign. Did she make the right decision? Should she talk to him, and get to the truth? This would be extremely risky.

It was the constant thinking about this case that had haunted her. Parts of it didn't make sense. Vance had been the main investigator on the case. Since he had more intimate information than anyone, she would have thought the prosecutor needed his testimony. In fact, her ruling had to be based on the fact, but behind the scene, she knew Xavier Vazquez was guilty. She had no doubt. If she ever had a case that might be reversed, or remanded back to her, this would be it. But . . . it had been over a year now.

Lost in her thoughts, she felt the boat sway as it reached the breakers. She needed to be attentive, and ready to help if he needed it. "Keep it straight."

"Don't worry. It's not bad today." Vance offered his arm to hold her steady. His brute strength never disappointed her. Nothing would be wrong with accepting it.

He felt warm and comforting as she melted in next to him. No one would see them out at sea. The boat quickly settled, as he powered up and raced away from the shore, and toward the distraction of Clearwater Beach. Still, she stayed close to him while attempting to force old memories out of her mind. Would it be possible to start over?

### 

Vance held Noella close to him. He needed no words to confirm her thoughts. Life could have been so different—if only. Why should he torture himself? It would be a long time, if ever, before he could afford to keep a woman like her happy. Rich girls were all the same. Until his dad died, he had certainly dated enough of them to make this determination.

It was not that they were bad, or even demanding. However, he knew it would only be a matter of time before money would ruin their relationship. He had no regrets in his decision to end their relationship. Yes, he hated it, and had to force himself to remember that true love sometimes required many sacrifices. Noella deserved so much better than what he could ever offer.

What he had never expected was her desire to become a judge in the same area he had decided to build a career as a law enforcement officer. Still, it was only to be a short term career since he had always wanted to go back to law school and obtain his degree.

He squeezed her tighter as he prepared to turn south. "I think we're far enough out to relax and take it slower toward Tampa."

"I agree. It'll be after dark when we make the marina, but this could be a good thing. It's still going to be up to you to get me back and forth from the courthouse the next few days until I can go back home."

"Are you sure that's what you want to do?"

"Yes, I might become a full time client for you. Well, not for you personally, but for your agency."

"I'm not set up for this, but I can make arrangements—yes."

"Hey, the sunset from here looks like it will be spectacular tonight. I'm going to see if I can find a good bottle of wine."

Vance considered how it would be nice to rest for

a while as they slowed to a leisurely cruise. They both needed to recover from the stress they had been under. Actually, he was amazed at how she had held up, considering the physical attempts on her life.

Vance studied the controls, and the electronics available. This boat had it all. He could only imagine the cost of such luxury. He soon had the boat off shore about two miles, and away from the normal boating lane.

Noella soon returned with a bottle and two glasses. "I know you say you don't drink much, but I think you can make an exception tonight, can't you?"

"With such a beautiful sunset, and a stressful day, yes, I think I would love to join you. Let me anchor first, and we'll stay here for a while."

Noella offered him one of those *I thought so looks*. "I'll wait for you on the bow." She motioned to a panel. "This is where the anchor is controlled."

As he secured the boat, he watched Noella in front of him, looking out toward the gulf. Even in the business suit she wore, he knew her petite body still packed all of the equipment that would excite any guy. He knew she needed to change, and hoped she brought adequate clothes. Since she had planned this all out before they left her house, he felt sure she did.

With the anchor firmly in place, Vance checked over the gauges, and breathed in deeply. The last two days had been a blur. Since she had information he needed to hear, this might be the best time to get it, and especially if she had several glasses of wine before they continued on their way to Tampa. Cruising into Tampa late at night would be the best strategy.

As she walked to the front of the boat, he studied her from behind. She remained the sexy little number he had dated several years ago, but now had a different exterior of protection around her.

He had got to know several judges over the last few years. They all had the same mentality. They had to keep a distance between themselves, and people around them, while maintaining an illusion of being friendly. Tensions inside the court room often led to problems.

Still, it was the body under the business suit that kept attracting his attention. Her firm butt was too much for the strict business attire to contain. Now that they were out to sea, she did need to change. But yes, he fully understood, she would need the suit to go to the courthouse tomorrow. But that was a long time from now.

Vance walked over next to her. While her long, blonde hair blew in the wind, and whipped her face, it seemed not to bother her too much. The dark, oversized sunglasses she wore had to be stopping them from stinging her eyes. This was something he had a problem with as the wind blew his hair into his unprotected eyes. He had no sunglasses with him. In fact, he had the same clothes, minus one t-shirt which had blood on it that he had on when he first met her coming into his office. Luckily he had removed his blue shirt the night before, and not replaced it until after fighting with the assassin.

He analyzed the questions he wanted to ask her, but knew to move slowly. She needed to see him as a friend first and foremost before layers of protective suspicion could be removed, and only then could he could obtain the answers he needed. He slowly slipped his arm around her as the first step in building such a connection.

The sun still had almost an hour until it would

disappear into the gulf. He scanned the horizons and studied a few boats off in the distance. Being out in the open presented some risk, but he assumed they had eluded everyone.

Noella slowly turned in his direction. "While the wine is still chilled, why don't you pour us some?"

"Sure, but we have a while until the sun sets. By the way, I placed your luggage in the main cabin. You might want to change to something more comfortable on the boat."

"You're right, but I didn't bring too much. If this drags on, I'll need to send for more clothes. How long do you think we can keep this boat a secret?"

He carefully considered the options. "I think for a while. I have some plans germinating in my brain, but I need to do some major research starting tomorrow."

"I know you do. While you're doing your job of investigating, I'll be in the court. I plan on working late, and this will make it hard for anyone to see me coming or going. While I'm inside the courthouse, I don't think anyone will be able to get to me."

"I know, but you can't live there forever."

"With the FBI and many other agencies working

on this, I hope it won't take long to get some answers. I know you're wondering why I wanted you involved in all of this."

"Yes, the thought has occurred to me, and you had also promised me some information on why you think I was framed."

"I did. Tomorrow I'll show you some classified information that I've discovered and I'll explain to you why I think so. For now, let me simply say the people who were pushing most for your removal are the same ones who are highly suggesting I resign from the bench."

Vance laughed, as he considered the officers in question. "That will definitely lower the number of people under suspicion, but we both know that these are also the ones who are the hardest to investigate."

"Tomorrow you'll have more authority to do so than internal affairs. Trust me on this. However, it might mean working closer with the FBI."

"Good, I'm looking forward to seeing what you have. Until then, I'll have to keep you safe." Now he had two reasons to do so. She was a client, and the holder of information that could clear him—not that he wanted to return to the force, he didn't. Being vindicated on his actions, however, was still important to him.

"Okay, I'll go change. You might want to check for something to eat also. I'm sure the refrigerator is stocked with food. It usually is." Noella edged away from his side, leaving a cooling sensation.

While they belonged together in many respects, why should he torment himself? It would never happen. "I'll check." He watched her walk away, leaving him again with his thoughts.

While knowing that he had a little time to kill, Vance turned his attention to the slowly developing sunset and his past. He had worked hard night and day on the force, hoping to climb the ranks. However, his real dream had been to make it back into law school. His admission into a night school program was to be approved shortly when all his dreams disappeared.

Xavier Vazquez had many people working for him. As the leader of a gang working in and around Tampa, he extorted many business owners who hired illegal workers in their business. Xavier had many nationalities running through his veins, and had said many times that he himself had no idea exactly what he was. He was the product of the street, and ignored by everyone until he found his strength. His loyalty was to people like him, and they respected him for that.

He could disappear easily on the backstreets until he wanted to make his presence known. Recruiting was easy for him. He offered a sense of community to those who were much like him. All he asked for was respect and total commitment, both of which he obtained one way or the other.

During his investigation, several members of Xavier's inner circle of thugs had been documented. A bust had been coordinated, and Vance was needed to cover a back alley. When several gang members surprised him by taking a different route, he found himself having to defend himself. After avoiding a barrage of bullets, he managed to fire off a full clip.

While one bullet had caught his left shoulder, he didn't pass out from the pain for several minutes, giving him time to glance back at those who had shot at him. In their midst he saw two young women standing by them. They were later determined to have been taken as hostages. How was he to know? Blood was everywhere. Then he remembered a new pain coming from the back of his head, and his world going blank.

He had replayed the scene over and over in his head forever. Yes, he made several random shots in protecting himself, but he never aimed for any woman, and had never seen any until after the gunfight. Even before he passed out, he could never completely say that he saw them bleeding, or showing signs of being shot.

Still, the evidence against him was hard to defend. His gun had been determined to be the murder weapon. Internal affairs had accused him of using excessive force, and shooting indiscriminately. He had no one to back up his story.

While the case would be hard to prove or disprove, he was offered an option to leave the force peacefully. Vance had spent six months investigating Xavier Vazquez and his operation. His knowledge of the case now appeared to be useless. The prosecutor must have thought he would be painted as a rogue, a dishonest cop, and a maverick that would make up things to get a conviction.

When Xavier was finally caught, and brought to trial, it appeared he might get away with everything. That was before the case landed in Noella's court. She denied one motion after another. Eventually she was able to send him away for twenty years.

Vance remembered following the case from the sideline, after he became a bystander, but one with the most intimate knowledge of Xavier's operation. At least justice had prevailed in sending him to prison. For Vance, however, it had failed completely.

Thoughts of being set up had occurred to him many times. He knew internal affairs had additional information about him, but would not disclose it. His case had been pushed to the side quickly. Who wanted to backstab him? Yes, he knew the force didn't want the public to think of them as trigger happy cowboys. Information on the people he shot appeared almost nonexistent. All were illegal immigrants. The only crimes they could be charged with would be assaulting an officer, Vance, with a deadly weapon.

The women were not armed. It was speculated by internal affairs that they were hostages. In truth, no one would ever know. But anytime someone innocent is killed by a police officer it's well known that their career is all but over.

Vance forced his mind to relive each shot he fired, slowing the sequence to a frame by frame accounting. His main target was a tall man with a grubby beard wearing a baseball hat. He had a pistol in his hand and was firing rapidly

Vance never had time to yell for them to stop, or that he was a police officer. It was possible they saw his uniform, or hat, but he could not be sure. His instinct was to fire back several times, and without focusing on what he was firing at. His bullets had apparently found their targets.

The bullet he had taken was only a flesh wound. Someone, however, had managed to get behind him, and hit him in the back of his head, knocking him unconscious. His next memory was waking up in the hospital with his reputation ruined. He had killed two innocent hostages. Still, were they really hostages? Internal affairs was quick to classify them as such. Yes, they were described as unarmed in the report. However, he always wondered if someone had removed their guns later. It could be possible.

He jerked, as he felt a hand on his shoulder. "What about the wine?"

"Sorry. I lost track of time," he said, as he studied Noella, who had dressed in a robe, as if she were ready to go to bed. Her hair was loosely blowing, and her makeup had been removed. This made her look frail and innocent, and so much different from the judge who ran her courtroom with the utmost authority.

"It's understandable. It's so beautiful out here."

"I'll be right back with the wine. I think it's now the perfect time to enjoy it."

### 

Noella thought she must be losing her mind. With someone trying to kill her, and after finally receiving the offer of protection from the FBI, she decided to rely on Vance, a guy who might very well be holding in his hatred of her, and waiting on his moment for revenge.

Call it instincts, but she didn't think so. Their time together may be history, but it was real. At least, it was for her. She had never been ready for it to end the way it did. One day she would find the truth of why he called it quits. The obvious answers were never the truth, and she knew it.

The only person that might know where she was outside of Vance was her dad, and she knew he would keep it a secret. He had his own world that he lived in, and never gave much of his time to her. She had known this all of her life. When her mother had died, her father had become a total slave to his work.

The waves had become almost nonexistent, as the boat rocked so very little that it reminded her of being in a quiet bay somewhere. It would be so nice to relax one day, and take a long cruise aboard it, and even better if she could talk Vance into it. She stopped. What was she thinking? She had no time for such a relationship, and probably never would as she pursued her career.

Noella watched him open the bottle of wine and hunt for a couple of glasses. She pointed to a small table with two chairs facing each other, which looked like the perfect place to sit and relax. She strolled over to it as he soon placed the glass of wine in front of her and slid into the other seat to join her. He then added a small plate of precooked shrimp he found—a perfect appetizer to enjoy during the sunset.

She lifted her glass, and smelled the white wine's crisp, fruity, yet tropical blend of aromas that was perfect for the Florida coast. After allowing the intoxicating wine to alter her mood slightly, she opened her eyes, and peeked over the top of her glass at Vance.

With him swirling his glass of wine, he appeared to have been studying her. He soon leaned in her direction. His eyes, which had the ability to change shades in different lights, suddenly added a mystical allure to their grayish-blue hues. Damn, if she could only penetrate them and find out exactly what he was thinking. Could he feel it, the connection, and the embers of a fire which never should have been left unattended?

The longer she waited for him to make a move, and to break his hold on her, the more intense his stare became. While the sunset behind her began to glow, the internal heat behind those eyes began to challenge its beauty and intensity.

As if in slow motion, he lowered his eyes to the glass of wine where he had obviously been preparing a speech for her. "They say wine gets better with age. Which may be true, I guess, but memories can be much better than anticipations of what might be. Do you agree?"

When did he become a philosopher? Still, he proposed a question, and one which must be answered before a toast. "I would hate to know that all I have is a memory, and I would also hate to know that all I had was a promise of a future. Perhaps it's best to have a blend of the two, and kind of like what a wine master hopes to achieve by blending grapes ready to be consumed now with those that will add complexities over a long storage."

"That brings it all to one all-important decision. How do you know when a certain wine peaks?" Noella studied his constantly swirling wine, and his intriguing words. The double meanings, and his teasing of *what-ifs,* left her wondering what he was trying to get to.

"When the time is right, they say the universe will let you know. Perhaps it might be what you would call *destiny.*" Suddenly memories of their past replayed. While drifting into those memories of so many years ago, she would have never guessed they would be having a glass of wine while discussing it.

"In any case, the bottle is open, and the present is at hand. Therefore, I think it's only fitting that we drink to the moment, and let the universe decide if it's a past, or a future."

"In such an agreement, I think I remember one toast that would fit. To this moment, and the moments to come." She raised her glass, and hoped he would support her hopes and dreams.

His intense stare and serious mannerism melted slowly at first, as his charismatic smile radiated a glimpse of a promise she could hold on to. "To this moment, to us, and to answers we both need." He extended his glass, as she wondered exactly who he had become. Would he share? How could she penetrate his armor?

"Agreed." Noella touched his glass, and studied the faint sound of glasses ringing between them. While a far distant sound from the wedding bells she hoped for one day, it did give her a small insight into her future. While she wasn't getting any younger, and she loved her work, a family one day was still what she wanted the most.

After taking a sip of the wine, Vance stood, and while he moved his chair next to her, he positioned it in the direction of the setting sun. He then asked her to stand so he could adjust her chair.

Moments later, they studied the same sunset, as the breeze increased slightly, and filled her nostrils with the crisp, salty gulf air. As the scattered clouds offered hopes of a spectacular burst of colors, she snuggled closer to him to accept his warmth, and security. This stopping in the middle of the gulf offered its own sense of security, but it also created an eerie feeling caused by those who wanted to hurt her.

She felt Vance slip his arm around her and pull her closer. It appeared that he had full intentions of her laying her head on his shoulder. So much for the professional relationship she had originally wanted. However, she had known from the beginning that there was a strong possibility this could happen.

The first glass of wine soon disappeared. He reached for the bottle, and poured the second glass for each, and thus drained the bottle. After turning the bottle in his hand, he examined the label, as if for the first time. "This is not bad."

Yes the wine was nice, but the connection felt even better. The sun would be disappearing before they finished this glass. Would he offer her a kiss during those final seconds? Would she stop him?

Seconds later, she rested her head on his shoulder, and became engaged with his muscles bulging under his shirt. The extra regimen he had as a private detective added a new layer of masculinity she would love to explore. Not having a steady boyfriend for a long time had left her wanting so many nights.

With maybe less than a minute before the sun disappeared, she studied the edge of the sun touch the horizon. Since this was always the ultimate moment in any sunset, she fixed her stare on it, and wondered what the night would bring. Would the afterglow give her any indication? While straining to keep her movement smooth and slow, Noella turned her face in his direction. She offered no resistance, and hopefully he would accept her consent. She still wanted him to make the first move.

Without hesitation, he accepted her gesture, and leaned in her direction. As he stopped inches from her lips, he was so close that she could feel his breath on her face. When the final inches finally melted away, she felt his lips graze over hers. She wanted more, but it was a start. Again, he barely brushed her lips.

To hell with this—she pushed against his, and transferred the heat she had been hiding into a fiery passion. Making out had always been a pleasure she enjoyed most of her life. The first minutes of questioning motives, and tentative explorations held a special tension she could not deny, or did she want to. While the afterglow sparkled, and fizzled, she created her own fireworks.

At last, the sun's afterglow drew to an end, as her head returned to rest on his shoulder. While the lights on her boat signaled their location, she saw no other boats close. She felt more hidden on the deck of the boat than locked away in a bedroom somewhere.

Vance soon moved slightly away from her. "Listen, I haven't had a shower in two days now, and I know I must have an odor. Keep your motor running, and I'll take a fast one." His voice resonated slow and clear. Did he think she had offered him sex? It was a kiss. Simply a kiss—or was it?

# Chapter 6

Vance couldn't deny his urges, or his needs that she had sparked inside him. Having an affair with a client was a definite no-no, and one he made himself promise would never happen. He knew how women in particular grew attached to someone providing them with security. But this was different. He had a history with Noella. He had forced himself to endure the pain once.

Still, the nights of suffering later, and second guessing had haunted him forever. A second chance—is that what this was? Later he would decide. For now, she had information he needed, and not to mention that she was a paying client. Okay, who was he kidding?

He staggered toward the guest cabin. The shower would probably be cold, but that may be exactly what he needed. He had to regain control. He needed to wash his clothes as best he could. It would be only after he delivered the judge to the courthouse before he could return to his place to pack some things.

After stripping, he stepped under the water which had some surprising warmth to it. The boat must have a solar heating system attached. Wow, this was some boat. He reached for the body wash, and went to work since he didn't know how much water was available. Feeling more human by the minute, he finished washing his hair and turned off the water. As he stepped from the shower, he reached for a towel.

Suddenly, a blast of lights flooded the room. What the hell? He fastened the towel around him, and ran for his pants where he had left his pistol. In seconds, he rushed to the front of the boat. The blinding light was pointed directly at him as he ran for Noella.

A voice boomed over a loud speaker. "Relax, folks. This is the coast guard."

Vance lowered his gun, but kept up his guard. The lights shifted to one side, and a guy in a uniform stood on the front of the ship. "We're making a sweep of the area, and just wanted to make sure you were not in trouble."

Vance yelled, as he pulled his towel around him, "I was actually trying to take a shower."

"We do apologize. This is not a good place to

anchor.”

“This was only temporary. We’re heading into the marina in a few minutes.”

“I see. We’re sorry to bother you.” The light turned completely off. “You two have a good night.” The boat surged around them.

Seconds later, Noella reached for him. “That scared the hell out of me.”

“Me too. I just knew we were facing another attempt on your life.”

“You don’t think they recognized us, do you?”

“I’m sure they recorded the name of the boat. If they check, it’ll come up as under my dad’s name. Since we have the same last name, I don’t know if they can connect the two or not.”

“In such a case, we need to disappear soon, but not too fast. I want to make sure they don’t see us heading out to sea.”

Noella appeared to be shivering in the cool evening breeze. He would love to share his towel, but that’s all he had to cover with. “Let’s go inside and get warm.”

“Sorry, they must have run you out of the shower.

I'll get another towel and help you dry."

Together they walked inside, and closed the door behind them. She stopped by the wheel. "You get dressed. I know somewhere we can go park, and where we won't be disturbed for a while."

Vance knew not to distract her. She had obviously piloted this boat before many times. "Should I ask where?"

Noella smiled. "A campground. Don't worry. It's not far."

Vance moved to the stateroom again to retrieve his clothes, but decided to do some checking. He soon hit gold; her father had clothes in the closet. He walked out carrying a couple of items. The boat had picked up speed as she ran for the south of St. Petersburg.

She laughed when he showed her what he had found. "I don't know how I'll explain it to him that his clothes had been stolen, but I'll think of something."

He waited for her to clarify. "Okay, maybe stolen is a bad word. I gave you permission to borrow them. How is that?"

"Better." He walked to one side and slipped into

the pants which were a loose fitting linen that her father must have used to lounge around the boat. In the cool of the evening they would be perfect.

Vance walked over to Noella and snuggled in behind her. "Do you want me to take over?"

"We'll be there in a few minutes. I think it'll be good to shut down, and keep the lights off until we decide to go on in to Tampa."

"I agree. We can talk some more, and maybe listen to some music if you want."

"I would like that. But first we need to anchor the boat."

Minutes later, he lowered the anchor, and secured the boat in a harbor next to the Fort Desoto campground. Yes, with only a few boats coming and going here, it would be a perfect place to hide while still feeling secure. When he pulled into Tampa later, he wanted the marina to be deserted.

He found a small light in the galley and waited for Noella to join him. The small couch also served as seats for a small dining table. This would be a perfect place to carry on their conversations. Now that all immediate dangers were over, he needed to learn more about what she thought about who was behind them. She obviously knew more than she was telling.

He moved to one side, and allowed her to sit next to him. As a single light highlighted her face, he noticed that she looked worried. He had seen the look before. If she lost her nerve now, then all of her hard work would disappear. Since it had happened to him, he wanted to make damn sure it didn't happen to her.

He knew that it was best to allow her the moments to work through her thoughts. It also gave him time to study her. Her hair had retained the beautiful, yellowish-blonde color he loved, but had grown longer. This fact she hid from most people, as she always tied it up into a ball in the back of her head when she presided over her court.

The single light made each strand of hair reflect its own glow, as they wove along her shoulders. While he had a strong desire to run his hand through them, he hesitated, knowing that she might consider it too personal. He still didn't know exactly where they stood. In one respect, he thought she was a client. In another aspect, he was ready to have sex with her by simply going to the bed directly behind them.

"Vance, as you probably know by now, I don't have many close personal friends. Being a judge doesn't allow much time for a personal life, and especially if you're intent on making sure you have your legal facts correct when rendering a decision. I want to advance to higher courts, and it will be devastating to have my court opinions overturned often. Do you understand?"

"I do. I went to law school for a while, as you remember. Being a judge is a huge honor, and I know you take it very seriously. I'm sure you have made the best decision you could based on the evidence."

"Most of the time I do. It's hard sometimes when you know the truth, and you have this major conflict inside you to follow the law, or follow the truth. It's a struggle."

"If I didn't know better, I think you must be analyzing your court cases and trying to decide if one of them has led to these attempts on your life."

She edged over closer to him. "Not exactly that, but related. I'm trying to understand why removing me would make a difference. What is different in the way I would rule? What case do I have a *personal interest* in?"

"When we get to the courthouse tomorrow, I plan on researching everything you have going, and I'll try to make some connections. It still remains to be seen how much help I get from the FBI, or the Tampa police."

Noella raised her head to rest on the wall behind her, but revealed her slender neck in the process. He wished she didn't do that to him. It looked so inviting, as her skin radiated with an innocent allure. The robe parted slightly, and gave him a view of her chest. A small nightshirt underneath hid little. He tried not to stare.

After raising his attention to her face, he focused on her eyes, which were closed, but reinforcing her innocent girl next door image. Her long eye lashes fluttered once, and then froze in place. Good, she was able to relax. He knew she needed this.

He watched her swallow once before slightly licking her lips to moisten them. Even without lipstick on them they resembled a smooth, velvety peach which was ready to be devoured.

He didn't remember moving forward, but still

there he was—inches from her lips—prepared to fulfill his inner wishes and desires. A small kiss wouldn't hurt. He had kissed her slightly earlier, and she didn't mind. In fact, she acted eager to go further.

He pressed his lips on hers with a small amount of heat to let her know it was intentional and exploratory. When he felt nothing in return, he started to withdraw from her, but then she returned the kiss. Not a passionate kiss, but a friendly peck as if he were a good friend, or a lover who only needed to be reassured of love without having to make love to prove it.

Vance turned more in her direction, and used his hand to stroke the side of her neck before feeling her silky hair. Hesitating briefly, he pushed it aside, and kissed her neck. The fleshy sensation coming from her warm skin made him want to nibble, to taste her, and to enjoy her earthly delights.

A slight moan confirmed she loved it, and thus offered all the permission he needed to continue. Nestling in closer, he devoured her scent, her heat, and her welcoming attitude.

She stretched slightly. "Vance, I don't want to

sleep alone tonight. I know this will be hard, but is it possible to sleep with me and not have sex tonight?"

Possible—yes. Probable—no. "What do you think?"

"I don't think I'll be strong enough to say no to you."

Placing the monkey on his back was not fair. Yes, he felt sworn to take care of her, but this would be asking too much of him. He was a man after all. "And what makes you think I would be?"

"I'm too stressed to give you my best. About the most I can offer is a body. Later, I promise, will be better. I simply need someone next to me tonight."

Vance understood. "I can make no promises, but I'm willing to try. By the time we get to Tampa we'll not have a long time to sleep anyway."

Vance had his hand massaging her shoulder, exploring every inch. It felt so natural. What would feel better would be dropping his hand to one of her breasts. However, in light of the current conversation, he tried not to think of how fantastic she would feel.

Thirty minutes later, his massaging had to be rubbing her shoulder raw. She seemed to be drifting in and out of sleep. Brief nightmares interrupted her, as she occasionally jerked back to reality. Inside his arms, he managed to calm her. Yes, she needed him.

A soft kiss on her forehead comforted her again. As she struggled to get closer inside his helm of protection, she placed a hand on his chest, where she returned the massaging motions he had been offering her. Memories of full massages they had given, and received years ago returned. He had almost forgotten about them. No wonder it felt so natural now.

Her firm exploratory hand did nothing to ease his growing urges. Getting a hard on would make it even harder to stop later, but some things were impossible to control.

With her last readjustment in his arms, he had new views of her breasts. Without thinking about it, he slid his hand lower. No reaction. Moving lower, he soon rested his hand on a breast where he studied its texture, and its firmness. The smooth feeling nipple had not been excited. While it felt so great to him, he wondered how she was enjoying it, if at all.

While attempting to convert to his part of playing protector, and not some fiendish maniac, he slowly raised his hand back to her shoulder. That is when Noella suddenly whispered, and surprised him in some ways, but not too much in others. "That felt good. You don't have to stop."

Confusing him was not a good thing, and not knowing what she wanted just added to his problems. He lowered his hand to her breast just the same, and started to pinch her nipple between his fingers—it responded this time.

Ten minutes later, he decided it was time to get underway. He kissed her forehead first, and then rubbed her shoulders, hoping to wake her slowly. "We need to make it to the marina now. I think it's late enough."

"Yes, but you feel so warm. Let me wash my face, and we'll get started. Cruising at night is different, but I've done it before."

"Me too. I'll raise the anchor, and get us back into the gulf so we can make it to the channel leading into Tampa. It will not take long to get there."

### 

Noella checked the ties after they docked in Tampa. It was not that she didn't trust Vance to secure the boat, but it was a habit her dad had taught her to recheck him when he cruised with her. "All secure."

"Yes, but we need to do one more thing. We need to cover the boats name so it will not be so obvious." He raised a mat which was used to walk on. "I think these will do."

Making the final adjustments, she walked inside again, and waited for Vance to close and lock the door. "Earlier I was sleepy. Now, I'm awake again. Shall we have a nightcap or something?"

"Generally I don't drink this much, but I understand the stress. Let me see what your dad has to offer."

Noella felt amused. "Dad uses this boat to entertain. The liquor bar will be fully furnished. Perhaps some brandy would be nice." Okay, she didn't want him to think she was turning into an alcoholic, but she needed to sleep, and she felt like she deserved it tonight, if not more so than any night in her life.

Minutes later he was digging into the choices. "He does have it well stocked."

She knew it would be. "Please turn off the lights, and bring it with you. I need to settle into the bed."

She didn't mean it to sound like a command, but she knew it did. Her nerves reactivated with a deep fear she had experienced earlier. Was this the best place to hide?

Walking into the master stateroom, she studied her dad's handiwork. One of the reasons she had become such a workaholic was because of him. He had never spent time with her. She respected him, but would love to know more about who her father really was.

Noella removed her robe and placed it on a side table. The light airy nightdress reminded her of how flimsy it was. While she never wore panties at night, she knew that if she could find the energy to slip back into them, it would provide one last layer of security tonight. She felt totally at Vance's mercy. Making love or not didn't matter tonight, she was too tired to object, and too tired to instigate.

After pulling the covers to one side, she slid under them and waited for Vance. An ever so light rocking of the boat indicated either a small wave, or him slowly walking on the boat. Another thought— someone else could be walking onto the boat.

She had heard that cops and private detectives made it a habit of sleeping with their guns. Did Vance? She prepared to call his name, but decided to wait and listen. Why was he taking so long?

Like a ghost materializing in front of her, she watched him float into the room. As a warm cozy heat flowed over her, she had to admit that she needed a man in her life. This truth was a tough fact to deny.

After pulling her dad's shirt over his head, he revealed a masculine allure that she knew she would have no defense against. Yes, since their last time together he had transformed into one hell of a well-tuned machine.

Would he still find her as attractive as he used to? She didn't have the time to hit the gyms. Still, she was young, and thankful for good genes. Without a doubt, she was getting aroused by his slow meticulous strip show. She couldn't take her eyes off of him. Was she getting wet? Oh yes!

Perhaps she shouldn't be staring, but she knew that he was dropping his pants next. Boxers. Yes, some things never change, as he wore the same style, and color—black. Try as she could, the fixation on his crotch area held her attention like a dog begging for a bone. His dick was large, and she could tell fully erect already.

He walked closer, and handed her a glass of brandy. With the intoxicating smell immediately enhancing her mood, she accepted the glass and folded her fingers around the base to heat the golden liquid.

Noella moved slightly to make room for him to sit beside her. "Did you turn off all of the lights outside?"

"Yes, and all is secure." He pointed to a side table where he had placed his Glock. "And this will be close by."

"I heard it was a habit of people who carry guns to keep them close to them."

"That would be correct." He raised his glass toward hers. "Since it's getting late, we need to drink to sweet dreams that will hopefully replace the events of today."

"That would be nice. Having you close will help. Thank you. I know this is not the normal request you receive." She watched him smile. "Okay. What were you thinking?"

"Just this. If I decided to bill you for this time . . .

it would make me a male prostitute, wouldn't it?"

"No, and I'm sorry if you feel that way. You're not on duty tonight."

"In such a case, I think we might have a good night."

Okay, she'd walked into that one. She lifted her glass, and swallowed the entire contents. "Let's turn the light out first."

She waited for him to place the drinks on the side table before reaching for the light switch. Several long moments lingered, as she waited for him to join her. Was he taking off his shorts?

The bed shifted as he lowered his body next to her. She rolled to her right, and onto his shoulder where her hand gently massaged and explored his skin. His chest muscles amazed her, with his tight skin reinforcing her desire to explore more.

She kissed his shoulder. Okay, maybe this was not fair. She had asked him to behave, so why couldn't she? And why did she have these conversations with herself? She knew. She wanted him.

She lifted a leg, and placed it over the top of his, settling deeper inside his personal comfort zone. While the thin nightgown stopped their skin from directly touching, the firm muscles in his leg transferred through nicely. This was becoming increasingly one sided. He remained still, waiting for her to make the moves.

As she dug in closer to him, she nuzzled his neck, and soon located his ear. She knew that if she kissed it, or made any advance there, he would have full permission to have his way with her. Should she? Hell—yes!

The response was as expected. His hand reached over, and massaged her shoulder for a second before lowering to her breast, where he slowly massaged her through her nightdress.

With all in motion, she lowered her hand onto his chest, and slid it lower. No boxers—good! Her hand soon wrapped around a full erection. Stroking him felt natural. Had it also grown over the years?

He turned toward her, and indicated that he wanted her to rise to help him remove her gown. With no problem, he pulled it over her head, leaving her fully naked next to him.

Protection—she had no protection. While he had

provided it earlier, was he prepared tonight? Either he was, or he didn't care, as he reached for her with his hand, and his fingers quickly playing with her folds. Should she ask now, or assume he did? She didn't need to become pregnant—not now.

When his finger found her magical bell to ring in an ecstasy she could not turn down, she forced her mind to clear. "I wasn't prepared for this. Do you have any protection?"

His finger stopped massaging her clit immediately. "Damn." He rolled to one side, and turned on the table light before opening a drawer. She heard papers being rustled, and heavy breathing. Then a quiet moment. "We're lucky."

Her dad had condoms stored on the boat! Well her mother had died a long time ago. I guess she would have to live with the fact that he was also a man. But come on—her dad?

Her mind cleared, as Vance turned to her again. His heat and scent reinvaded her thoughts and body, which was now out of control. How long had it been? Too long. She reached for his dick again to verify she was not dreaming. The pulsating joy stick in her hand needed to be directed to where it was needed—inside her.

Vance rolled her to her back, and leaned over to kiss her before applying a new found force and passion. She opened her mouth, as he used his tongue to explore her. The full length of his body paralleled her own with millions of sensory receptors charging and firing electrical bolts throughout her body.

His dick now pressed against her leg. She spread her legs further apart to make it easier for him to climb on top. His fingers spread her again, as he dipped in a finger. She felt extremely wet and ready. She needed him now, as she pulled him over her.

After centering her, she used her hand to guide him home. Without hesitating any longer, he slipped inside and immediately thrust over and over, and as now a demon possessed. She raised her knees higher to give him more access to her body, and enter her deeper.

She could enjoy this all night, and had no intention of stopping any time soon. A wave of heat building inside her continued to build, which signaled that she would be coming soon. The rest of the world blurred into oblivion, as she locked all memories into the deepest closet of her mind.

After grabbing his powerful ass with both hands, she pulled him tighter, as if begging for every single ounce of his energy, and being. She never considered herself to be a screamer. This time she had no control over it. Thankfully the marina was vacant, as she yelled repeatedly. Damn, she loved sex.

She relaxed finally, but noticed the slow in and out actions of Vance, who patiently waited for her. If he could help her come again, he would be extraordinarily gifted. She increased her grip on him, and welcomed the encouragement. A few minutes later he had accomplished a miracle.

She couldn't move a muscle, as her body collapsed from exhaustion. She owed him a climax, but he would have to do the work. She didn't fight him, as he rolled her on her stomach. With her legs spread, he centered her. She trusted him to penetrate her pussy from behind and not try any kind of kinky anal sex.

Seconds later he entered her. The direction and feel were different. New sensory explosion lifted her to a new height. This time he hammered much more than previously. At this pace he would have to come soon.

Again she had a mounting wave of ecstasy. She concentrated on it, and hoped it would be soon enough to capture the moment Vance would come.

Vance had muscle she couldn't believe rubbing against her body. He slowed to measured, yet powerful thrust. Yes he was coming, and she would be soon behind him. She didn't scream this time, but disappeared in a garden of love where she would love to live forever.

**Chapter 7**

Vance woke early and checked to see if she was still sleeping. He had phone calls that he needed to make to others who worked either for him, or with him. People he could trust. The contacts he had inside the police force didn't want to be caught helping him. He understood why, and it was also to his benefit to keep such trusted friends protected.

Securing the perimeters was his first duty for the day, as he quickly walked about the marina. He also had to make sure the docking fee was paid so that no one would question the boat being there for a while.

He knew that finding a secure phone to talk would not be hard since the local gas stations sold disposable ones. While the courthouse was not far away, it was too far to walk on the street with the judge. Once he had her inside, he would have plenty of time to arrange further security.

Astor Clark worked with him before, and had the perfect vehicle to get her there—a work van with no lettering on it. No one would ever notice them coming or going. He made the call, and arranged the transportation without a problem, or having to answer any questions.

As soon as she was inside and safe, he would continue on to the parking garage and retrieve his truck. It had additional equipment and firepower that he might need. After returning to his office he would have to think where to hide it for a while. He had a couple of locations in mind.

Next, he wanted to meet detective Johnson, one remaining friend on the force, somewhere secure. A bar a few blocks from the station would be perfect. This off the record info would be his best source of information. Johnson answered quietly. "Hello."

Vance decided to get straight to the point. "I think you owe me a beer."

"I might."

"Yes you do, and the last time I bought the rounds." Vance hung up. Enough said. Johnson would know where they had met last time.

After drifting along the dock, Vance studied the area, and how being right under their noses could possibly be the best place to be. They would, he hoped, never look for her here.

After carefully making his way back to the boat, he waited for signs of life before he entered the boat. He felt like all was secure since the inside the boat remained quiet. After the last few days, Noella needed all the sleep she could get. A lot depended on what she could find out today.

When he eventually entered the state room, he found her curled into a ball, and looking like the angel he remembered. Slipping in beside her was so tempting, but no, he needed to get prepared for the day.

As he moved toward the galley, he wondered what he could find to eat. He quickly located some bacon and eggs. Yes, her dad did keep it prepared for guests. Even canned biscuits were available. Good—a full breakfast would be nice.

As he finished cooking, he looked up to see her joining him. "This smells too good to stay in bed. How long have you been up?"

"A few hours. I needed to line up a few things. I dropped money into the payment slot on the marina board, which will help make sure we have no questions there."

"Good. They usually give everyone time to pay in the morning."

"Do you think they'll recognize the boat?"

"Sure, my dad pulls in here all of the time, but it's usually occupied by guests and clients of his." She smiled. "Relax, they will suspect nothing."

After placing a plate of food in front of her, Vance studied the robe she had wrapped around her. Underneath, he remembered the woman he had made love to the night before. How could he forget? However, today she was a woman he had to protect until he could find out who was behind the attacks.

He reached over and offered her a hug. "We need to get you into the courthouse early and before the traffic peaks. I have us a ride lined up, but it's not exactly a limo."

"I understand. With the manpower investigating this, I think this *having to hide out* will be over quickly. I hope so anyway."

"Listen, after I drop you at the courthouse, I have to take care of a few things. You'll be well protected inside."

"I agree. It would be impossible to get to me with the courthouse security as it is. Should I ask what you're up to?"

"Let's call it research." He turned his head to avoid any further inquiries.

She appeared to understand. "I think perhaps it's best I don't know. You will be careful—right?"

"Being careful sometimes means being the aggressor. Some things in this town only happen with the permission of a different type of authority." That was about as close to telling her what he had to do without spelling it out.

"It sounds dangerous." A look of concern registered, as she spoke.

However, he quickly dismissed it with a kiss on her cheek before he added, "It's nothing for you to worry about. I'll see you by lunch."

As Noella returned to the stateroom to get ready for work, he prepared for his day. An electronic ear piece in the lapel of his shirt could be obtained easily when needed. A spy glass with digital video recording capabilities always came in handy, and could be stored in his pocket. His iPhone was loaded with applications he needed, but most important was the firepower he carried.

His favorite Glock fit into his shoulder holster, one which he examined fully before moving on to the next—a light back up ankle revolver. Inside his belt were a collection of knives, several of them Japanese throwing versions he had practiced with for years. In his heels he carried a canister of tear gas. Not sure if he would ever need it, but still a surprise that might come in handy one day.

He glanced around to make sure Noella was not close by, as he added a bullet proof vest. He wanted to be prepared, and while Noella might not like it, she would also be wearing one today as she entered the courthouse.

As he finished, she walked in. "I think I'm ready." She glanced at his bag he had carried with them from his truck. "You look like you're prepared for war."

"I think it's best to be prepared." He tossed a vest on the table. "This might not look fashionable, but this morning I insist."

Vance watched her squirm, but eventually

consent, as she opened her jacket and started to remove it. "I never thought it would come to this."

"We need to hurry. Our ride should be here in a minute. And . . . one more thing. Don't use your phone today. I purchased you one to talk to me with. Your phone can be tracked and someone can locate us with it. I have turned it off." He handed her the phone, a simple call feature only style.

"I wondered why no one has called me."

He looked into her eyes, and immediately read the fears she tried to suppress. "I'll take care of you. I promise."

Vance ventured from the boat first and walked along the dock. With nothing appearing to be out of order, he went back to help Noella. He stayed close to her, as if they were a couple instead of a target on the hoof. He quickly ushered her along to the van waiting for them, where they disappeared seconds later.

Vance didn't feel the need to make introductions as the van sped along the back streets toward the courthouse. When the van stopped, he spoke slow and deliberately to his friend. "Keep your eyes open, and I'll be back in a minute."

"You got it. All looks clean, Vance."

Vance escorted her to the front door where a uniformed police officer, who immediately recognized her, waited for her to check in. He watched her glance back at him before saying goodbye. "Take care and I'll see you later." Without attracting any more attention, he walked back to the van. Good, they had not been noticed.

It was a short drive to the International Plaza and the parking lot where he had stashed his truck. He needed his truck, and access to more equipment. While he knew the perfect place to store it later, he first needed to make a stop to see what was going on in the police station. His normal beer joint also sold breakfast where his friend in the force could possible give him the leads he needed. This *off the record* report might be far different from the official word he would receive later.

Finding places to park where he didn't have to pay high parking fees was a challenge for some people, but not for him since he lived there. This one spot that he pulled into was always available. He locked his truck and started to walk.

Minutes later he saw the side entrance to Duffy's Bar and Grill standing open. He didn't hesitate as he walked in and headed to a back room where they had some pool tables. He quickly joined Johnson and waited for him to finish the breakfast he was apparently enjoying.

Johnson, as always, was a no nonsense type guy. "You're late."

"Sorry, I don't seem to have the little blue light to get around traffic anymore." Vance considered ordering, but assumed that he would not be there long.

"Everyone is wondering how in the world you landed this case. I'm sure you know by now that the only help you'll get will be very superficial. You really rattled some cages when you left."

"I'm just looking for the truth."

"You know that might be a life-long quest." He finished the eggs. "It appears that someone has placed a price on the judge's head. They won't tell you all of this, so act like you don't know if it comes up."

"Any idea who?"

"Best guess is that its gang related. Check the cases she tried involving RICO."

"That will be my next stop. But . . . what about word on the street?"

"No one is talking, and as you know in Tampa we have so many splinter gangs. This will take a while. If you plan on asking questions you know you'll not be received too well."

"It seems I have a way of not making many friends anywhere these days."

He slipped Vance a small piece of paper. "These are the guys asking the most questions in the department. They're not too happy about internal affairs around asking questions again."

"Thanks. If I have problems, I might be calling on the cavalry."

"In your case you might get an army of one." He shifted the bill in Vance's direction. "You know some of the regulars in here in the mornings are on the force. Keep your ears open, and your head down, my friend." Vance watched Johnson stand and walk away.

Vance decided it might be worthwhile to stay for a while and see who showed up. After he found a seat closer to the grill, he started drinking coffee and planning his day. He only had so much time.

When he was finally convinced he was wasting his time, a few officers walked in. They acted cocky, and like some of the totally arrogant bastards that ruined his career. Since he didn't know their names, he decided to keep his head down and enjoy the coffee. While he was close enough to hear what they would be talking about, he doubted they would give any full disclosure of their activities, but any clue would help. He had little doubt these were the ones Johnson had warned him about.

The first words exchanged were naturally about the Tampa Bay Buccaneers and how bad the season was so far. With them all expecting it to be much better soon, he heard enough to know they were all betting on the games. Illegal, of course, and since they were sworn to uphold the law—what a joke this was. These were the guys who gave the rest of the force a bad name, but managed to get guys like him that worked hard canned.

After they ordered breakfast, he finally heard words he wanted to hear as they discussed what they were assigned to for the day. Without giving specifics, they were all working gang activities of some kind.

Several times he heard them whisper too low to understand the words, but loud enough to indicate they were concerned about being overheard.

If it was a gang related threat on Noella, these guys knew much more than they would ever admit. These could very well be the guys who framed him. He had to know more, but for the next thirty minutes, he heard nothing new. He waited for them to leave first. He had a few names they called each other by. That would do for a start. He would be at the police station after lunch, where he had been promised help. Oh yeah, he would see how that went.

After leaving the grill, his next stop had to be his office to pack some clothes, and add some supplies that he might need. He didn't have a lot to select from, but would manage on what he had. One day his life would turn around. He was getting closer, and he expected the fee he earned on this around the clock service to pay well. Since he knew it would be mostly from the feds or the state, he didn't feel too bad by taking it.

His office looked exactly as he left it. The door was locked, and a single light was left on from earlier.

Still, he had a habit of checking it out before he settled in. He had converted one side office into a bedroom, which also included a small bathroom. This is all he had available. Since it was zoned for multiuse, he didn't break any laws by staying there.

The arrangement also saved him money, which he would need if he decided to go back to law school. Even if he never received his degree, the contacts there would provide an endless source of work for his PI business later.

He glanced at his phone and saw no messages. Okay, so he wasn't extremely well known. Or, it could be that everyone called him on his cell, which he had now turned off to keep from being tracked. Since he was now inside his office, and it didn't matter, he turned it on, and ran through his voice mail.

He had received fifteen calls, and all of them from law enforcement officials wanting to know where he was. He knew they had a job to do, but so did he. He understood how they wanted to talk to him, but since he was working for a judge, they would have to take it up with her. Again, this would not make him many friends. However, until he knew who was really behind this, he trusted no one.

After packing everything into a large backpack, he turned on his alarm system and stepped outside. Ten feet later, he heard his name being ridiculed from inside a side parking lot. He stopped and waited for the person to walk out to him. Since he stayed half-hidden, and appeared to be the only one there, Vance stepped closer. He carefully surveyed his surroundings, and prepared to draw his weapon if he felt any need to do so.

A plainclothes officer of some kind stepped closer to meet him. While his face looked slightly familiar, he offered no badge or name. "I was hoping you would show eventually. There are a lot of people looking for you."

"I can imagine. However, I'm only concerned about one person here, and she wants to make sure certain people don't find her. I think it's understandable that she trusts no one right now."

The stranger never removed his dark sunglasses. "How in the hell did you end up with this case?"

Vance felt annoyed, but knew to be patient to see why he was being contacted so discreetly. "Just lucky,

I guess. Do you care to tell me who you are?"

"It's not important right now, and since I think this is a better off-the-record chat. Of course, if you're not interested in some information, I can walk."

"Information is always nice to have, but the source is more important. It appears I receive a lot of bullshit information."

"I know you don't trust people inside the force, but there are a lot of honest, hard working people there."

"I never said there weren't. I'm sure you heard the story about one rotten apple."

"And that would be a job for internal affairs, and not a cowboy on the loose, wouldn't you think?"

"Yes. That is, if they would do their job. However, in my humble opinion, I tend to believe that they haven't."

"Much like assholes, we all have one. The judge is a friend of mine, and I'm not the enemy. To be able to help, I do need information to work on."

"So do I."

"I'm open. Tell what you have, and what you need. I can make no promises."

"Understood. The case file collected on me would be a great start."

The guy's stalling techniques escalated as he stated the obvious. "You know much of it is classified, as it has to be."

"So, you're not here to really offer me help. I think we both know that now. So, what is it you want from me?"

The stranger offered a full smile, obviously not wanting to lose the last bit of connection he had with Vance. "I'll level with you. The people who are targeting the judge might also be the same people you need to talk to about your own problems. That's about all I can say at this time."

"That would not surprise me. Bad apples tend to show up in the same spot in the barrel. Can you give me some names?"

The stranger's cocky grin turned into a small chuckle. "I think you already have some names. Breakfast was good this morning, wasn't it?" As he turned, a business card floated to the ground, one which the stranger didn't even pretend to notice. As he turned away, he waved goodbye over his shoulder.

Vance retrieved the card, and read the name on the card—Kirkland, the head of the department of internal affairs. This was much more serious than he assumed. Was this guy one of the men who worked under Kirkland, and thus blowing a whistle on his boss?

After turning the card over, Vance glanced around before he read the note on the back. Black Knight. That was interesting. Could this be a code name for a case someone was working on? He would find out more later when he had access to the files at the police station. He memorized the code and discarded the card by tossing it into a small puddle of water.

## Chapter 8

Noella worked hard to clear her schedule as much as possible without causing an unnecessary disruption to her flow of cases. She made a complete list of each trial in front of her, or would be in front of her soon that she knew about. Slowly, she started eliminating cases that were too small to cause such a major threat on her life, which were many of them.

She was left considering about ten major cases when Vance arrived. Her assistant ushered him into her chambers as she had been instructed. Noella hoped she could hide her attraction to him, since no one needed to know of their affair. Trying to treat him as an independent private detective, or body guard would require will power, and lots of it. She wanted to hug him, and exchange a kiss, but not now—later.

She assumed he would understand. "It's good to see you made it back. We have some work to do." She pointed to a chair in front of her.

After her assistant closed the door, Vance walked

over to her chair. "Being a judge suits you."

Noella felt a small rush of pride. "I'll take that as a compliment. Vance, what have you found out?"

"I had an interesting visit this morning outside my office. It appears you have some friends in internal affairs that care about you."

Should she try to hide the fact she knew who he must be talking about? "I see." Looking across her desk at him felt strained, so she stood and walked around to the adjacent chair next to him.

"I have a few names. Is it possible to cross check their names with the names of witnesses named in pending cases you're handling?"

"I can do that, but it'll take a little time." She leaned closer, and glanced over her shoulder at the door behind her. A quick kiss wouldn't hurt. He obliged, but retained the heat she knew he packed inside. Okay, later would be better.

"I'm going to the station when I leave here after lunch. What do you have for me that I need to check on?"

"When cases are assigned to me, but are still under investigation, some of the information is not presented to me until later. It could very well be that the police and the prosecutors know something they're not telling me. It could be for a reason such as trying to obtain more proof, for example."

"That will be hard for me to obtain, since they know I'm working for you. They don't want to screw up a case and have it thrown out."

"Yes, it's a tricky situation we all find ourselves in, but this is the perfect reason to have you look at it in an independent mode."

"Trying to isolate a crime against you and a crime they want to keep from going to trial is more than tricky. I don't expect they'll be rolling out the red carpet for me." Vance shifted in the chair. "What . . . based on publicly available information, can you give me?"

"This." Noella reached for a file. "I think these are the only cases that would really matter, and result in trying to have me removed. It's not much to go on. I'm sorry."

The intercom box on her desk beeped. "Judge, there are some men here from the FBI who want to see you."

Noella stood and straightened her suit as she walked to her large desk across from Vance. "Send them in."

As the door opened, she stood and walked toward them while extending them her hand. Vance remained in his seat, but cradled the file she had offered him. "Hello, gentleman. I thought you would be by soon."

"We received word earlier that you were in your chambers. You really need to trust us, and let us provide you with our protection."

"I have protection, but I appreciate the offer."

The agent passed an unimpressed glance at Vance. "We might need to discuss this in private."

"He's planning on leaving shortly, but I want him to hear what you have found out first since he's in charge of my protection for now." She kept her voice authoritative, and one they would not fight with.

"Being part of your protection, and part of an investigation are two different things."

"Understood. First, what is it that he can be told?"

The two men glanced at each other. "We think a gang out of Miami that specializes in extortion and violence for hire has been paid to put out a contract on you. It doesn't have to be murder, but any kind of removing you from office will do."

"And have you found them and arrested those responsible?"

"First, we would need proof, and that will take some time to obtain. This group is very loosely organized. The only way to stop this is to identify the source of the money offering the reward."

She motioned toward Vance. "I would like for Vance to help. He's not a police officer, or FBI, but he has experience in working with ICO cases in the past."

"He was also released from the Tampa police force for his actions."

"In America, I thought a man was innocent until proven guilty." Vance spoke smooth, and calm, but forceful.

As the agent started to reply, Noella intercepted. "I'm appointing him as a special investigator for me. As such you're expected to give him your full support. Is that clear?"

"Clear." He nodded to the other man.

###

Vance parked his truck a block away from the

station, and set the alarm as he walked away. He felt like he would have no problems now that he had demonstrated that he was on to any tracking devices, but he knew to recheck when he returned.

With the soured face on the officer working the front desk confirming his expectation of what kind of help he would really receive, Vance decided to waste no time in getting to his point of being there. "I think we all know why I'm here, and I do expect full assistance as I was promised."

The officer grinned, as if he was preparing for a battle.

Vance raised his voice to make sure his intentions were extremely clear. "I need all files on these cases, and I do mean all files. Additionally, I want a room with a computer that has direct access to anything else I need."

"It will take a while for us to arrange it."

"Really!" Vance retrieved his iPhone. "Even a police officer can be charged with obstruction of justice."

"And who do you think you're calling?"

"FBI. I would estimate you have ten minutes to

comply before you go to jail."

The officer glanced at the iPhone. "You know, files do go missing from time to time."

"Tell it to the judge. You'll be standing in front of her within an hour."

The police chief suddenly walked into the room. "Hello, Vance. I thought you would be here soon. I hope you receive all of the help you need. I like the judge, and I want to get to the bottom of this as much as anyone around here."

Vance didn't smile. "That's funny, since I was just told by this officer not to expect much, and that all the files I want are . . . *probably missing.*"

The officer acted differently as he was being exposed. "Chief, we all know this guy will say and do anything to save his rear. I didn't say anything like that."

Vance lifted a recorder from his pocket and prepared to hit the replay button. "Chief, I think you'll like this."

The front desk officer turned red face with anger, as he cursed under his breath. "Damn you! You're wearing a mic in the police station!"

The Chief raised his voice as he pointed to the officer. "That does it. I want a staff meeting now with everyone in this office. Am I clear?" The chief kept his finger in the officer's face. "After the meeting, I want to see you in my office. Don't blame Vance since he's here at the direct request of the judge. You'll have some explaining to do." The chief looked at the request on the desk. "I'll see to it you have these as quickly as possible. However, on the direct access to all police files, I'll have to have you monitored. I think you understand that."

"Understood. However, I want someone who I can trust. Is Nelson available?"

"I think it can be arranged. My assistant will set it up while I have a meeting with everyone here. The sooner you finish your work, the better." He walked closer to Vance. "We have a detective assigned to this case also, and I would appreciate anything that you can tell him about whatever you discover. That is, if you want to really be a team player and have the judge's interest at heart."

"As long as this is a two way street."

The chief nodded his approval. "I'll see what I can

do. I want to get to this bottom of this. I also want someone from internal affairs to come see you. Also, before you leave here, I want to see you again."

"I look forward to it."

Minutes later, he was escorted to a private office with a computer. Before he could settle in, Nelson walked in. "I see you're already plucking feathers from the roosters here."

"I thought it might be the best way to get them crowing. Since we have a lot to do, let's get started."

Nelson smiled, as he pulled up a chair.

"Good, here is what I need to cross-reference. I need cases that the judge will hear within the next six months that has any connection with a mob or racketeering group of any kind. While we're at it, we need to compare this with any cases that I was involved in also."

"Why you?"

"The judge could not give me specifics, but she thinks the people behind this might also be the people that framed me."

"We all know the case that got your ass canned, but Xavier Vazquez is serving time on that one."

"Let us start with that case. Is there any chance it will be remanded back to the Judge?"

A few minutes later, Vance obtained the status of the case. "Okay, it looks like it's being heard on appeal, and that the judge is hoping to render a decision soon. Yes there is a possibility, but no one will know for sure how the judge will rule. I don't think the judge will tell anyone until the decision is made. Yes . . . there is a small chance it could happen."

"I wonder if someone knows more than we do on this. It would be good to talk to the prosecutor and see what he thinks."

"That could be an interesting conversation. The prosecutor wanted to use you, but after leaving the force in the midst of the shoot out, they were scared to do so. They were afraid any evidence you had would be turned against them and be used to show the information they had was tainted."

"We both know that would be a lie."

"After being dismissed for using excessive force, they would still plant the possibility that it was obtained illegally."

"We both know the judge knew the truth. She had to take that into consideration when she made her ruling."

"Under the law she is required to ignore this fact. However, I'm sure this is one of the points made in asking for a retrial."

Vance stretched as he considered the various ramifications. "I think I understand now. This would be a perfect reason to make sure she wasn't on the bench when it was reheard."

Nelson maintained a solemn stare. "But now prove it."

"We have our work cut out for us, for sure." Vance tossed the other cases to one side. "I still want to concentrate on this one for now."

"I'll try to help. What is it you need?"

"Two things. I need to have the prosecutor tell me the truth on what they know or suspect."

"And the second thing?"

"I need to go to the prison holding Xavier Vazquez and ask him some questions."

"I kind of doubt he'll see you."

"He might, that is, if we dangle the right carrot in

front of him."

"Such as?"

"If he feels like he was set up, and can see a connection to my being set up, we might share a common adversary."

"Do you really think he's dumb enough to believe that shit?"

"Maybe not dumb enough, but mad enough if he thinks he was sold out by someone else. It could be that someone who supported him changed ships and did do that."

"So you still think there are some dirty cops involved."

"I think so more now than ever." Vance pointed to the computer. "While I'm checking to see what is in the computer, can you see if the prosecutor on the Xavier case can join us?"

"I'm sure he has already been made aware of being called, so hopefully he'll join us soon. What else?"

"The chief mentioned they have a detective investigating these attacks on the judge, and I think it will be good to see what he'll share with us."

"Since he has an interest in solving this case, I'm sure that will be no problem."

Vance felt like he might be getting somewhere. It was time to push. "I need to talk to internal affairs, and see what they know."

"We both know that will be the hardest part. You might want to ask to see them last."

"No, but since we know that, I think we need to get the request in as soon as possible." Vance smiled. "I saved the easiest part for last."

"Such as?"

"When we were about to be paired up, we were going to be working the gangs in Tampa. Someone had to take over for Xavier once he was sent off to prison. I want to see any files on this case. It could be he's doing the dirty work for Xavier."

"The investigating officer assigned to this case will not like you sticking your nose in his business. This is the detective that was most instrumental in having you removed."

"All I can say is—tough shit."

"Anything else?"

Vance felt his muscles tightening, as if he was

prepared to do battle. "I think that will do for a start."

## Chapter 9

Noella wanted answers, and asking pointed, direct questions was not a problem for her. Whatever they knew, she wanted to know. But unlike most people who stood in front of her, the FBI agents had been well trained.

She immediately dispensed with any formalities. "I'm going to ask some questions, and I don't want any sidetracking or incomplete answers. Tell me what you know, and what you suspect."

"What we know is that your life is in danger. The hit men that have been hired to abduct you are part of a lower class cartel. They were obviously hired this way to make tracking who hired them impossible."

"I'm sure with all of your intelligence, and tracking abilities that you can connect some dots here."

"We're working on it, but it will take some time. It would have helped if we could have taken them alive." The FBI agent's words sharply criticized

Vance's actions.

"If you're referring to Vance killing the two assassins, I think we both know that he had no other choice. Let me remind both of you that when you're under imminent danger of losing your life that the law is very clear that you can defend yourself. The more I see firsthand what Vance is up against, the more I wonder how justified it is to label him as a rogue cowboy on the police force. When this is all over, I think a complete review of his earlier problems should be conducted, but that will be later. For now, tell me what else you know."

The two agents passed a quick glance to see who would talk next. The tall one doing all of the talking until now continued, "We received word that a contract was placed on your head from a source inside a gang in Miami, one which is not my district."

The other agent entered the conversation. "We have a theory, and at this point it's simply a theory. We hope you'll keep this quiet until we find out more."

"I'm listening."

"As you know, the court system is over loaded,

and the longer it takes a case to come to trial, the more difficult it is to prosecute a case."

Noella waited for him to continue. "Please continue."

"We have also heard that many gangs across the state are now working together to create havoc in the courts. If they can have several judges removed, or feel threatened, they can cause a major backlog that will serve them well."

"So you think that I'm not the only judge in danger."

"We think you may be the first."

"And you have not warned any of the judges about this theory."

"This is a relatively new theory, and we'll be contacting all judges soon based on this attack on you."

Noella wasn't buying it. "That might explain one attack, but not several. Have you been able to get a positive ID on those that Vance shot?"

"The men that Vance shot had no identification on them, but had a few Mexican pesos in their pocket. A tattoo on one of them marked him as part of a Mexican cartel. While we have the Mexican authorities doing more research for us now to try to identify them, my best guess is that they were picked off the street and sent on a somewhat suicide mission."

"That's scary. There has to be one person who is masterminding this."

"That could be one of several people."

She knew he was stalling. "Such as?"

"If we gave you those names it might taint your ability to rule on some cases. Are you sure you want them?"

"Your point is well taken." Yes, there appeared to be many ways to have her removed from a case. "It's your job to find out who is behind this, but it's my job to stay alive. I also think you need to give me any information I need to guarantee my safety."

"As we stated earlier, we can provide you with around the clock security if you wish."

For a second, Noella realized they were telling the truth. Should she tell them her suspicions of the danger lurking inside the Tampa police department? Rather than offer her protection when she was receiving the threatening calls, they only suggested she step down.

Knowing that she had to work with the officers on many upcoming cases, she decided to hold her words. Some of the conversations they had earlier returned. She knew they had their hands tied on many things, but had lost several cases lately due to lack of evidence.

As she replayed her history, she watched the agents studying her, as if they had noticed a weakness in her stand to use a private detective. "Gentlemen, here is what I'm up against. I had threatening calls for awhile and no help from anyone. I now hear you say you knew of a threat, but didn't tell me beforehand, or provide any protection until I was attacked. And now . . . you want me to trust you!"

"We're doing our job."

"By the book."

"Yes."

She couldn't control her laugh. "And you consider Vance as one who does not play . . . by the book?"

The agent demonstrated his training in keeping a straight face, while showing no emotions in his response. "The call is obviously up to you. We'll do what we can, as this is an ongoing investigation."

"I want you to tell Vance everything you know or suspect. He'll need this information to protect me until you have completed your investigation, and we determine who is behind this. I hope you understand me."

"We'll do our best."

###

Michael Hodkins, the state prosecutor during the Xavier trial, walked in to join Vance. He looked like a lawyer with his standard pin striped suit, starched white shirt, and solid colored power tie. The highly polished black shoes added the final touches to his appearance. The stern look on his face quickly set the tone that he was all business, and was not one to be dictated to. While he reported to the state district attorney, and had his own rules to follow, he had made it clear earlier that he did not like Vance.

Vance cleared his throat and held out his hand to shake. This was one challenge he welcomed. While his personal case was not the reason for the interview, it did give him more time to study this asshole.

He must have gone to a special school to learn how to be arrogant. "I was told to come see you, but before we start, I'm sure there's not a lot I can tell you since this is an ongoing case."

Vance decided to stay firm and in control for as long as he could. "I don't intend to ask you anything unethical or illegal, but I do expect your cooperation and the truth."

Apparently, any confrontation only pushed Michael into a more confrontational stance. "You can expect all you want, but we both know I don't have to tell you anything at all."

"I think we both can agree that Judge Peterson has been attacked twice and that her life is probably still in danger."

"And from what I've heard, she could be much better protected by the FBI than an officer forced out of the Tampa police force."

"Forced might be a good word, but I doubt if we'll ever agree on the reason for the force." Vance fist tightened, as he fought for control.

"Internal affairs investigated your claims, and found nothing. Becoming dedicated is one thing, killing innocent bystanders, hostages, is another."

Vance still had a hard time deciding if this guy

was truly believing this shit he was spewing, or part of the conspiracy that burned him. He decided to play a different card. Since Michael was already getting mad and obviously not going to tell him anything, he might as well add to the heat and see if he would say anything he wouldn't otherwise.

Vance leaned forward. "We both know that is a lie, and one day, hopefully soon, I'll prove it. We both know that my testimony would have helped in putting Xavier away, but you decided to not use my testimony."

"After your stunt . . . you've got to be kidding? The defense attorney would have ruined our case."

Vance leaned closer, intentionally invading Michael's personal space. "I made a mistake last time by staying quiet. I won't the next time. Michael, you can count on it soon."

"What do you mean . . . soon?"

Vance knew he had hit a nerve. "I'm sure you've heard the case is being remanded back to Judge Peterson. This time, I can make a statement in the court, as a friend of the court." Vance hoped his bluff would stun him.

However, while Michael looked indignant, Vance noticed the small expressions of concerns. "What have you heard about it being remanded?"

Vance decided to play out his hand. "Perhaps you would like to tell me what you know."

"I can't discuss this case with you, and you know it."

"Sorry, I think that's what we've been discussing for the last fifteen minutes."

Michael turned toward the door. "I don't think this discussion ever happened."

"Oh, it did. My next stop will be to see Xavier."

"I don't think I can allow you to do that."

"I don't think you can stop me. I'm a private citizen now. And by the way, I've been appointed by the judge as a special investigator for the court."

"Really?"

"I don't know exactly where your allegiances are, but I can tell you the safety of the judge is my top one now."

Michael snapped back as he sneered. "You don't really think Xavier will talk to you, do you? There are reasons you don't know as to why you were not put on the stand. My intentions are to keep Xavier in prison where he belongs. Don't get me wrong, I know you have a job to do in protecting the judge, but I have one also."

"I think I have the right to know why you never used my testimony."

"That . . . you'll have to take up with the judge, and since I was sworn to never discuss it with you or anyone. It could ruin my case."

Was Noella holding back on him? Was he being used? He forced his emotions to stay in check until he saw her again. "Believe it or not, I want to see him in jail forever also. I worked on this case for over two years."

Reluctantly, Michael offered one bit of hope in mankind, not to mention the DA's office. "For what it's worth, the information you obtained was critical in putting him away. However, it could never be used."

Vance maintained his stance directly in Michael's face. "The question remains as to why you think I'm guilty of anything but doing my job."

"Vance, if I could prove you were guilty of anything, I'd be prosecuting you. As far as the case against you for excessive force, I don't care. It's not my job to charge you with anything. It is my job, however, to send Xavier away for good."

"At least we have one common goal."

"For what it's worth, I doubt Xavier is behind any attempts on the judge. We have him fully monitored. And if you do get to see him, be warned that your conversation will be recorded."

"I would fully expect that it would." Vance decided to push. "We both know, or suspect someone will step in to take over his operation. Do you have any upcoming cases that I need to be aware of?"

Michael derisively glanced at his nails. "We're gathering information on some pending cases, but nothing I can disclose. Sorry."

"I guess I was wrong. I thought you would be interested in keeping the judge safe."

"Believe me, or not, that's what I hope I'm doing. Is there anything else?"

"Not for now, but I'm sure we'll talk again."

###

After making notes, and using the computer to check on cases assigned to various officers and detectives, Vance built his list of names that he needed to talk to. Several of them worked the same type cases he had. They were also the ones who turned on him earlier. But why?

Detective Fedder, a guy he had worked with several times, walked in. "Hello, Vance. I see you have found a way to get involved back in cases you need to walk away from."

"How is that?"

"You're the one with blood on your hands from innocent bystanders."

"You don't believe that. My shots only hit the people I fired at—not the two women."

"Ballistics confirmed they came from your gun."

"But not that I fired them."

"The gun was in your hand when you were found."

"I was knocked out and I woke up later in a hospital with a concussion. Since you know that, I would hope you would do your job and find out who did that to me."

"As I have testified, I entered the alley where the gunfight had happened, and I saw no one but you and the dead people. I even thought you were dead at first."

Vance kept wondering if Detective Fedder was the guy who hit him. A cop hitting a cop would be hard to accept, but it remained one possibility. "So how did you explain my concussion?"

"We all assumed you must have fallen and hit your head, which knocked you out."

"And you believe that?"

"That is what I testified to."

It felt like Vance was talking to the proverbial brick wall. "We all know someone is trying to either intimidate or possibly kill the judge. Are you interested in helping me or not?"

"I think the best way to do that is for you to step aside, and let the Feds do their job. If the judge feels intimidated, she might need to reconsider her job. This is a tough job that she has. She will always have threats against her."

"Well, at least we understand each other. She mentioned that she received no help from the police department earlier."

"That's not necessarily true. As you might

remember, we work best when we're not noticed."

Okay, he had information he was not going to share. However, with full access to his files now, Vance knew he would know more soon. Perhaps a trap was being set for the follow up gang leader.

"For now, I'm working for the judge. I really would hope that you would want to help."

"I never said that I would not help. I simply have a job to do also."

###

So far he was receiving no help from anyone. The last person to come to see him would be the hardest to get anything out of, but would know more than the others—internal affairs.

As the head of Internal Affairs walked in, his large frame and commanding attitude flashed an immediate image of hate toward Vance. Vance knew that facts had been hidden from him when he was asked to leave. Agreeing to the terms of his termination had haunted him, and if he had the chance to do it over, he would fight it. Still, he had to focus on the case at hand. He needed to see who was behind the attempts on Noella. He decided to wait for the guy to speak first.

"I was told you wanted to see me. I think you might know who I am." He handed Vance his card.

"Yes, I know who you are."

"I don't have much time. Tell me what you need from me."

"The truth." The times of being intimidated by internal affairs were over. Since Vance was no longer on the force, this guy had no power over him.

"Why do you think I would lie to you?"

"Maybe not lie, but not tell the whole truth." Vance raised his voice in a measured show of strength. "First off, I would love to know why the police department never afforded the judge any protection."

"We're doing a review of this case. She did file several requests with the police department, but was not able to substantiate her claim until now. There may have been some misjudgments, but nothing outside the police protocol."

Vance remained determined to get answers. "Since I'm now charged with providing protection to the judge, I need to know what you know to do my job. What can you tell me?"

"I think it's pretty much assumed by everyone that its gang related, and tied to some case she is, or will be handling. This is something we need to handle, and not have you involved with."

"Since the judge hired me, it's obvious that she does not trust the police force to do their job."

"I hate to hear this, but I understand. Vance, I'm not the bad guy here. I like the judge and want her to stay safe. I promise many people are working on this behind the scenes, and trying to connect the dots isn't as easy as you would think. We hope to have a break in this case soon."

"Me too. I trust you'll let me know if you have any news on who is behind this."

"As soon as we can get to the bottom of this, I suspect there will be some arrests. While some people assume that it's a case involving the judge, it might be part of a larger plan to get rid of many judges."

"I've heard this theory already, and do not buy it."

"Why is that?"

"I spent too much time on the street working the gangs around Tampa. They're not that coordinated."

"If you know something we need to know, we

would appreciate it very much."

"As you said earlier, it's only a hunch, and nothing that can be proved."

"This is going to become a nightmare of a case before it is over. You could've gone to jail for what you did, and don't forget it. So, be careful for what you ask for."

"Are you threatening me?" Vance felt ready to defend his rights, even if the guy in front of him acted tough and intimidating. Vance was no longer under his control.

"No. I was just making an observation."

"You know that this isn't over. I think that's all for now. There will be another day—count on it."

Vance shut the door behind him after he left. So much for being nice and playing by the rules. It was crystal clear that he needed to gather his own information. What was it that everyone wanted to hide from him?

## Chapter 10

Noella reviewed her calendar again. She had no intentions of having her schedule disrupted any more than possible. While many lawyers asked for continuances to gather information, a few asked to have their case heard earlier in the hope to have their client released from jail. There was nothing specific that she could see that would make someone want her to step down. She tried to think of what would make her rule any different than any other judge.

She decided to call Darlene, her assistant in and talk about the cases. This was the one person that legally she could discuss her cases with. Her opinion might be very helpful.

Darlene shut the door behind her, as she entered. "How are you making it today?"

"About as expected, I guess." Noella twisted in her seat. "Did you have any problem rearranging my schedule?"

"Not at all. I think every attorney in town knows

what's going on. They have all expressed their support of you, and wanted you to know that they are there for you in any way they can be."

Noella closed her eyes for a second, as she reflected on the facts. "Darlene, give me your honest opinion. Am I being overly paranoid on this?"

"Are you kidding? After being shot at and almost abducted—not at all. I'm surprised you're not hiding out somewhere until this is all over."

"I'm thinking that's what someone wants to happen. I need to find out who that might be."

"Are you thinking this is an impending case you'll make a decision on, or one you'll see later?"

"That's the part I don't know, but it would have to be one that I'm specifically targeted to handle."

"We know all of the ones you have been assigned. We also know the ones you have ruled on that are being remanded to you, which are very few."

"I think we have these fairly well documented, and I'm sure the FBI knows these. What high profile case is in the works that I might be receiving?"

"You need to call the district attorney or the attorney general's office on this one."

"That might be an interesting call, since they also know what's happening to me. They might even be considering reassigning some cases away from me and never let me know they did."

"That's a strong possibility."

"In such a case, we need to concentrate on one thing, which is why would I rule any different than the next judge."

"Since you've had very few cases remanded to you, which is a huge accomplishment, I can make some quick calls, and see if there are any which might be. The chance of getting any concrete facts is going to be hard."

Noella knew of a few cases she would hate to see returned to her. Xavier was high on the list. He had stared directly at her the entire trial. She had no questions in her mind that he was guilty. She knew the evidence against him, but she couldn't understand why it wasn't presented. The prosecutor must have known something they weren't disclosing.

Still, on this case he wasn't part of a larger gang. Could he really reach out from prison and cause her problems? Vance knew this case well. She needed his help here, but she knew to be careful. She didn't need to disqualify herself from rehearing it if she had to.

Darlene pointed to the clock, which indicated it was already six, and an hour after she should have left. "How long are you planning on working tonight?"

"Maybe another hour. I know you must be tired. When you leave here, be sure to take an officer with you to your car. I don't know how crazy these people are, or how far they'll go to make their point."

"Trust me, I will." Darlene stood and walked toward the door. She was also planning on going to law school next year.

"Good, I'll be leaving in a little while."

"Is Vance coming to get you?"

"Yes, and I need to give him a call. By the way, let me give you a new number I'll be using until this is over. Vance purchased me one of those disposable phones."

"Really. This is starting to sound like a cloak and dagger episode." Darlene stepped closer. "I hope it's okay to ask, but how is Vance doing these days?"

"He's staying in shape, and doing the best he can with what life has dealt him. He's still a mystery to me. Perhaps I can unravel some of it while he's protecting me."

"I hope so. I always liked him."

A slight defensive surge hit her. She knew Darlene had the looks to attract any man, even Vance. But who was she fooling? Her time together with him would be short lived. He would soon be free to spend time with anyone he wanted. She definitely could tell no one, even Darlene, that she was sleeping with him again.

As Darlene focused on her face, Noella suddenly realized her hesitation in answering was sending the wrong message. Darlene knew her too well, and perhaps even better than she knew herself. She had never really gotten over Vance. "What?"

"If I didn't know you better, I would have some naughty thoughts right now."

"I don't think I would use the word *naughty,* but we both know this is a very stressful time for me."

"As always, you know my lips are sealed, but I'd love some details later."

Noella knew she had to have her help in keeping this contained. Her reputation was at stake. "You know I have to keep my private life exactly that—private."

"I fully understand, but if I'm going to run interference for you, I need some kind of heads up, don't you think?"

"Okay, Vance is providing twenty-four hour coverage for me right now. It's complicated."

"I bet it is. You know you're playing with fire."

"While this might look like a scandal, it's not. What we had before is a simple love affair that ended like many do."

"But we both know many will question this if he was a major witness in a trial you were hearing. And now he's back in the picture as someone is trying to have you removed."

"Crazy—isn't it?"

"So why did you get back in touch with him?"

"It was not an easy decision, but he might be the key to my problems. However, I might get a chance to correct an error I might have made."

"Really."

Noella decided to confess. "To make sure no one would say I went easy on him during his case, which was destined to be in front of me, I may have overdone it to make sure he was removed, and thus not tried in my court. Since Vance thinks he was framed, and has never stopped trying to prove it, I'm now convinced that he may have been, and even worse, that I was used to make sure he was asked to leave the force."

"If true, that would be terrible."

"Yes . . . and I don't know how to offer an apology, that is, unless I can play a part in helping him find the truth and thus help him get exonerated."

"How do you plan to do that?"

"Vance is now being given access to files he never could see earlier. As smart as he is, I hope he'll find what he's looking for."

"I hope it works out for you."

"Thanks."

## Chapter 11

Vance arranged for use of the work van again which would hide their getaway from the court house. He saw Noella waiting on him with a guard by her side. She looked so professional in her business suit. Had she changed totally, or was part of the fun loving girl he remembered still hiding underneath it all?

He rushed over to her and escorted her to the van ahead of him. As soon as they were seated, the van sped off. It would not take long for them to disappear, and they could be dropped off by his truck a few blocks away. They would be out and hidden in seconds, and if anyone was following them, they would never see the drop.

Vance finally turned to face Noella. "How was your day?"

She shrugged. "I have nothing much to report. I really found out nothing new. What about you?"

"It was much as I expected, no one wants to share anything with me that they don't have to. They're doing only what they're specifically asked to do and volunteering nothing," Vance said, as he glanced behind the van for any cars that might be following them. "However, I may have hit one sensitive nerve today with the prosecutor on the Xavier case."

"Why? What did you find out?"

"I bluffed and told him that I heard the case was being remanded to you."

"Interesting. And what did he say?"

"It wasn't what he said. It was the reaction on his face. He knows something is up, but refused to volunteer what it is. He did say that Xavier was closely guarded, and that he thought it would be impossible for him to be behind all of the attacks. It was, however, amusing that he wanted to stop me from talking to Xavier."

"Are you planning on trying to see Xavier in prison?"

"Yes, tomorrow morning. I doubt if I'll learn anything, but I will definitely get the interest of several people. And especially if I drop some key words that only a few will know about."

"So you're planning on baiting some people to

come out into the open."

"Have you ever noticed how some people say things that they normally never would until they get mad?"

Noella hesitated. "I hope you know what you're doing."

"I think if word gets out that the prosecutor is wanting to stop me from talking to him, Xavier will want to hear what I have to say."

"Don't you think he'll have his attorney with him?"

"Maybe and maybe not. After all, I'm not on the force anymore. I'm just a normal citizen making a social call."

"Not exactly. You were a material witness in his trial."

"A small correction. I was a potential witness. There is a big difference."

"I see your point, but if the case is remanded to me, you could be called this time."

"That will be highly unlikely, since the defense will question why it was not presented the first time."

"Point taken."

"Other than smoking out who is behind these attacks what else do you have on your mind?"

"The truth, and nothing but the truth." Vance motioned to a stop coming up. "Be prepared to move fast. My truck is close to here."

## Chapter 12

While Noella pondered what Vance had on his mind, she knew that it would be best that she didn't know some of what he had planned. She had to trust him.

Later, as Vance had her rushing toward the boat, she noticed several guys studying them from across the harbor. Did they recognize her, or was it her dad's boat they were studying? The three men were too far away for her to recognize them.

Her heart started to beat rapidly as she ducked inside. Vance placed a small revolver on a side table, as she collapsed into the small sofa. "Stay here, I need to do some checking on a few things."

"Yes. I saw the men staring at us."

Vance reached over and kissed her forehead like he had done so many times years ago. "I'll be back shortly." Instead of immediately leaving the boat, however, he went to search it first. He eventually opened some electronic gear, which he must have been using to check for bugs before he smiled and silently left.

The quiet settled around her like a large blanket, as she intently stared at the pistol. Did he think she would really know how to use it? How long did he plan on being gone?

Time advanced slowly. What was he doing? She tiptoed toward a port window and glanced outside. She knew he would not approve, but the waiting was haunting her. She could see no one, and the only sound she heard was a sea gull squawking above her.

She felt the slight shift in the boat. Someone was walking onboard. She started to yell out, but stopped. What if it was not Vance? She walked over to the pistol and slowly wrapped her hands around the stock. It felt much heavier than she had assumed it would. She glanced to see if it had a safety. This was stupid. How would she know? She had never fired a pistol before. She waited.

Something creaked, as the boat shifted again. There were no waves in the harbor, unless a boat was maneuvering out of a slip. She wanted to yell out, but couldn't.

Vance walked through the door and shocked her with his sudden appearance. He quickly grabbed the pistol. "Careful, we don't need to explain any gun shots."

"You scared the shit out of me!"

"Sorry, but all is cool. I recognize one of them. They were just curious I'm sure. I wasn't spotted, but we do need to be discrete when we come and go."

With the impending pressure off, she felt her muscles relax as she fell in his direction. He felt so powerful just holding her. She never considered herself a weakling before, but she had never been the subject of an abduction, or an assassination before either.

"Let me see if I can find the tequila and make you a drink. I think you're officially off duty now." Vance grinned, and acted like he wasn't worried at all. It must be nice to stay so cool.

"If I keep this up, you'll soon think that you're taking care of an alcoholic."

"Not at all. If I was in your position, I think I might be having a drink or two also."

Noella motioned to the seat beside her. "Aren't

you going to join me?"

"Maybe later on tonight. I need to do some work for a while first."

A small wave of anxiety passed over her. "You're not going to leave me here alone, are you?"

"I'll have someone posted right outside while I'm gone."

"Where are you going?"

"Let me call it on the street research. It appears they may have more information about what's going on than the police."

"Isn't that dangerous?"

"It's what I did for years until I was knocked off the force. I still have some contacts." He grinned. "Don't worry. Tonight I'm just doing a drive through certain areas. I can find out much of what I want to know from the truck."

Noella finished her drink and found a new level of courage. "I want to go with you."

"I don't think so."

"I want to see what you're doing, and what I might be facing. I insist. It will be easier to protect me with you than to leave me here with someone else.

You said you weren't going to leave your truck."

"This is a part of town I don't think you've ever seen."

"Then it will be a learning experience for me, and something I need to see firsthand. And I definitely don't want to stay here by myself."

"I'm just going to do some drivebys tonight to find something I can use. If you keep your head down you can go. I agree, you might need to see a side of town you might not know about."

"Exactly where are you talking about?"

"The backstreets around Ybor City. This is a place that many illegal and homeless congregate. It's prime property for gangs to recruit, and drugs to pass. Life there is very hard for those who find their way to it. Xavier capitalized on this area, and I want to see who is running it now."

"And you can tell this by driving through it."

Vance glanced away as he attempted to explain. "Sometimes rival gangs leave subtle, and then again, sometimes not so subtle markings of their turf. With Xavier gone, I'm sure we'll see a new leader taking over."

"Since you're not on the force anymore, why would you want to know this?"

"The one thing that Xavier will want to know is what is going on with his old turf. I think he'll be willing to talk to me if I can provide him with some information he wants."

"You know your conversation with him will be monitored."

"Damn, I hope so. The police use coded words to coordinate plans, and the gangs use the same methods, but with different words. I plan to introduce a little cross breeding that should prove to be interesting."

"What exactly do you plan to accomplish out of all of this?"

"I want the truth, which includes someone talking to me. I'm sure Xavier thinks someone set him up or turned their back on him. While I'm not sure if he's behind this or not, he might know something useful we need to know about. The trick will be getting the information from him so that it's not intercepted."

"But what if he is behind this?"

"If he is, he'll want to know what I know. I fully expect him to try to play me."

"But don't you suspect that he'll have his lawyer there to monitor your questions."

"Exactly how this works out remains to be seen. I think it all depends on what kind of message he receives from my activity tonight."

"It will be interesting to watch you in action, but scary. You said this would only be a drive through—right?"

### 

Vance adjusted the mirrors and the hidden cameras covering his rear. This truck was a work of art that he felt tempted to show off tonight, but he knew better. He needed to find something he could use to get Xavier to talk to him.

He had seen the code word *sidelines* and knew it was related to operations in the Ybor city area. Pedro Sanchez's name was very familiar in the area. He was the one person who helped set up Xavier. This was always interesting since he also got away with hiring illegal workers. Supposedly, he was forced to do so by Xavier.

Due to a lack of concrete evidence, trying to prove that Pedro was also connected to Xavier's operation had been impossible. Vance always had his doubts. Any witness they had located who was willing to talk quickly disappeared. Pedro ran a construction company which hired many people on a project by project basis. Without the protection of Xavier, he would be a sitting target. There had to be someone else he was dealing with now to supply his labor force. This name would be very helpful to drop on the street.

This new leader would be the person that Vance would suspect the most. Whoever it was could be holding down the fort until Xavier returned, and might even be a left over member of his gang.

Vance turned to Noella, who was buried in the sock cap he found for her. He did not need anyone to identify her where he was headed. "I'm sure you've been to Ybor City before, but this will be a new side of it for you."

"I've lived in the Tampa area for a while, and I've had cases in front of me which involved this area."

Vance smiled. He knew that analyzing it in court and seeing it in person would be different. Minutes later, he turned down a side road and slowed to a crawl. The lighting was bad, but all looked still and quiet.

Suddenly, he saw a girl walk out of the shadows. Her short dress and high heels would normally look out of place, but she was obviously here to get business. A slow moving truck was like a beacon for her.

"I assume that must be a hooker." Noella glanced sideways. "Do you know her?"

"Not yet."

The young, Latino looking girl appeared to still be a teenager. She stopped walking next to the sidewalk, as Vance pulled his truck closer to her and rolled down the window. "You're a little young, don't you think?"

The hooker smiled as she slowly sucked on a finger. "Why? Do you want to be my daddy, and spank me for being bad?"

She needed much more than a spanking. He knew just the person to help her, but later. He needed information before he scared her off. "That's interesting, and you might need a spanking." He stopped to glance around. "Are you freelancing, or do you have a pimp?"

She appeared to pick up on his sideway glances.

"Hey, are you a cop?"

"No, but let me say that I've been around for a while." Vance watched her eyes dart to the shadows from where she had ventured. Vance knew where her pimp was. It was time to bait him out of his cover. He opened his door and walked closer to her, as he spoke louder. "Get your things together. I know a place you can stay and receive some help."

"Help? What help, man? I'm doing like fine here on my own." She backed away from him.

His baiting worked, as a tall, black guy slowly walked out of the shadows. "Hey, dude, what's your problem? If you like what you see, you need to pay for it. If not, you need to move on. We have a business to run here."

Yes, this guy thought he was a real bad ass, but so far this pimp didn't recognize him. "I don't need a woman, but what I need is some information." Vance walked closer in a direct show of defiance.

"Information also cost money, dude. Just don't go messing with my ladies." The pimps gold teeth sparkled in the dim light.

"It's amazing the cops have not put more slime

balls like you in jail."

"I have plenty of protection. I'm not worried about nothing. So, dude, do you want some fine ass, or not?" The black guy flashed his gold capped teeth again. "Of course, we need to do this where I can keep an eye on you, now that you're thinking of making off with my honey."

"No, what I think is going to happen is that you're going to answer some questions for me–for free. And then she'll also receive the help she needs."

"Ahhh, man, I don't think you know where you are. This is my turf." Two other black guys soon joined him. One of them held a short steel bat in his hand.

They spread to both sides, as Vance stepped forward. "Well, I haven't had any exercise today. Are you sure you want to do this?"

The answer came quickly as the guy with the bat swung first. He missed—Vance didn't. As he moved closer, Vance's quick right broke the guy's nose, sending blood flying. Before this black guy could recover, a flying kick landed additional damage to his face, and sent him down for the count.

The other black guy rushed at him with a knife. Vance grabbed the back of his hand, and forced him to drop it, snapping a bone in his arm in the process. When this guy hit the ground, he screamed from the pain before Vance struck him one more time, knocking him out.

The pimp went for a gun, but Vance retrieved his Glock first and pointed it directly in his face. "Are you sure you don't want to answer a few questions?"

The pimp offered a nervous laugh. "Hey, man, I'm like a walking, fucking encyclopedia. Who in the hell are you?"

"Your girl is obviously not from around here. Where, or shall I say who, obtained her for you?"

"Man, you know I can't answer a question like that."

Vance pulled the hammer back. "Since you pulled a gun on me, I'm fully justified in pulling this trigger and then letting the girl answer for herself."

The pimp's eyes widened as he apparently understood that Vance was not kidding. "I don't have a name. He drops off the girls and I toss some money. It works best that way. I think the girls are daughters of the men he hires to work for him."

"Who is this *he*?"

"Hey, dude, like I don't know his name, but he took over for Xavier a year ago."

"Is his name Pedro?"

The guy's hesitated, but soon answered, as the gun moved closer to his face. "Do you know him?"

"I think everyone knows of him. One more question before I let you go. You said you had protection. I need a name."

"I don't have one."

"Okay. How do you know who to trust?"

"The black knights are the only names I know. I promise that's all I know."

Vance surveyed the area, and knew the disturbance would be called in. He would have company soon. "Get the kid off the street, and find yourself another line of work. The *black knights* are going down."

Vance walked back to his truck and slammed the door behind him after he jumped into his seat. This direct intrusion should send a loud message to everyone. He had made his presence known.

As he sped away, Noella screamed at him. "That was more than a drive by I think! What in the hell did you do?"

"I made a quick side trip—sorry!" Two blocks later he made a quick pull to a stop. "Now the fun will begin."

"What do you mean?"

Vance pointed to a screen. "I left a remote camera behind. It will be interesting to see who shows up."

Noella leaned closer to the screen where she saw a detective's car pulling closer to the camera. "Oh my god."

## Chapter 13

As Noella walked on her boat, she had many questions circulating in her brain, and very few answers. A detective was on the take. Why didn't the FBI know about this? She had to know if this was related to her threats. While she still couldn't connect the dots, she shouldn't have to since she was a judge, and not in law enforcement.

Vance had handled three gang members as if they were kids. If she wasn't so damn scared, she would be damn mad at him for putting her in such a situation.

As she breathed in deeply, she wondered how she was ever going to prove this. "Okay, now what do we do, Vance?

"Since we now have a chip in the poker game, we could play our hand, or we could try to get a few more chips."

"Pedro was the victim in the case I handled. Are you telling me that now he's the new Xavier?"

"For all I know, he could have been Xavier's boss

from the start." Vance rubbed his chin. "I think we'll find out more when we get to the truth about a case being built against Pedro now. At the same time, I think we'll see those who are trying to protect him. It sure would be easier if the good guys wore white, and the bad guys black."

"In your opinion, is this tied to the attacks on me, or not?"

"It's too early to tell, but I hope to smoke out some more information when I go to see Xavier tomorrow."

"I would love to be in on this conversation, but that would be so inappropriate, and dangerous to my rehearing of the case." The more she started to think about it, the more she began to realize she was getting too much into investigating a crime.

"I do know enough about the law to understand what kind of position this is putting you in. You need to trust me to do the right thing without asking too many questions."

He was right—*damn him.* "The FBI wants you to keep them informed. What are you planning on telling them?"

"The truth. That is after I discover what it is."

Noella breathed deeply, as she glanced around. She felt a strange sense of security in her boat with Vance around. "I'm hungry."

She watched Vance smile before he walked to the kitchen. "It appears my services as a chef are also needed."

"I guess we can call it part of the twenty-hour service plan." That did not come out exactly as she intended. She hoped he didn't consider having sex at night part of his paid services.

Vance turned toward her and fixed his gaze on her face. She froze, as he lingered, intensifying the focus of his wolf-like eyes on her. "I'm sure you'll get your money's worth."

Okay, so he did put her in her place. She needed a drink. "Can I make it up to you tonight by making the drinks?"

"It would be a start."

Noella could only guess what he meant by that. Until moments ago, she wasn't in a romantic mood. His eyes changed everything, however, as her heart continued to beat hard and fast. The questions about their past would have to wait. She only hoped she would have the chance later to ask questions she wanted answers to.

###

Vance studied the choices. A salmon steak looked good as he searched for something that would compliment it. Unless he could get someone to break the silence that had baffled him for the last year, he knew he would never determine why he was set up.

The evening was still early, which was good. It would give him plenty of time to talk to Noella. She had also promised him more information, and he had been waiting patiently for her to provide it.

As he waited, he had no clue how long Noella planned to disappear in the stateroom. She had been given a brief view into a world she had been sheltered from. He knew that after a failed abduction, and an assassination attempt, she had to be getting the picture of just how brutal that part of the world could get.

The smell of his cooking must have drifted into where she was since she rushed to where he was busy at work. "Wow that smells great. Maybe you need to consider being a chef."

"I love to cook, but not all the time. I hope you like it since I added a lot of spices."

"Oh, I can smell them. How long before we eat?"

"It's almost ready. Why don't you pick the wine this time?"

"Deal." He watched her turn and walk to a small wine cooler. The small robe she had brought with her was thin and clung tightly to her body. With the shape of her rear catching his attention immediately, thoughts of making love also replayed. He fully expected tonight to be a repeat of the previous one. He felt no need to rush it along since they had plenty of time.

As she leaned over to study the lower level of the cooler, her robe parted, and revealed her legs up close to her hip. He saw no panties. His dick went hard as he stared. While she had to know she was doing this to him, she played innocent.

She selected a long bottle, one which had to be a German, white wine of some kind. While accepting this short period of time to enjoy the better side of life would be nice, he knew that his money would never allow for such extravagances.

Noella held the label for him to see. "I'm sure this will be good. Let me open it."

As they enjoyed the food in almost silence, Vance realized she had an agenda much like he did. It was soon going to be a give and take time. She had secrets, but so did he. His, however, would remain that way forever. It was best that way.

The wine soon disappeared as quickly as the meal. With no maid service, he knew the plates had to be cleaned and replaced. As he stood, she grabbed his hand. "No, since you cooked, it will be my job to clean up. I've already made myself comfortable. Maybe you would like to do the same?" She winked.

*That wasn't playing fair. Was she interested in a quickie before they went to bed?*

Noella continued to wave at him to get him moving. "Go on. I'll even fix us an after dinner drink." She winked again.

"I never wear pajamas, if that's what you're referring to. I think *this* is my normal comfort."

"And you never walk around wearing only your boxers when you're at home?"

Now she was waving a large red flag in front of

his bullish manhood. "Are you sure that's what you want me to do?"

The sincerity in her eyes answered for her.

He allowed his focus to drop from her eyes to her chest where the robe had slightly parted enough to show cleavage, but no nipples. She looked extremely inviting. *Okay, why don't I just go ahead and surrender?*

Vance reached over, placed his hands next to her neck, and gently glazed her skin before he pulled the robe together. "We need to talk for a minute first."

"Yes . . . yes, we do." She leaned closer to him and kissed his cheek. "You are so different from any guy I've ever known."

"I think every guy and girl have differences. Sometimes they are easy to see, and other times you have to hunt to discover them."

She appeared to be happy with his answer. "I would love to go out on the front of the boat since it's nice outside, but I think we both agree that might not be such a good thing."

"The least amount of attention we create until this is over, the better. We can stretch out on this sofa and do just fine I think."

"It also converts into a small bed for guests. But . . . we do have two good beds onboard."

"I think it's fine just like it is, but before I give you a strip show, I do need to check the perimeters one more time before we settle in."

"As you wish. I'll have your drink ready when you're satisfied."

*Why am I fighting this so*? He forced himself to concentrate. "It'll only take a few minutes." He knew the fresh air from outside would help clear his head. He needed to concentrate on how to pull the information he wanted from her. He had to see which officers she suspected to be part of this. While he had some names, he needed to know if she had others to add to it.

"I'll be back in a minute." He leaned over and kissed her forehead, much as he had many times before. Seconds later, he was walking the outside of the boat. He moved slowly, as he studied the other boats around him. Only one appeared to be occupied, and that one by an older couple. Being quiet was a good thing.

Thoughts of the day so long ago when he had decided to leave Noella resurfaced. It had been seven years since then. While he still regretted it, he knew it was something he had to do. At least her life had turned out good. He would have hated for her life to be ruined by the scandal caused by his dad.

After walking to the end of the dock, he thought of his mother. She had moved to Atlanta where her sister had a business. The move had been good for her, and had helped her put closure to his father's death, and soften the blow of being penniless.

Vance had never seen his father bet, but the records spoke clearly. He had gambled his entire wealth away on the internet. At first, Vance did not believe it. While he had always hoped that someone had to be making this up, and lying about his dad, the information was too hard to dispute.

He breathed in deep and wiped the memories from his head. He was proud of Noella. She had finished law school, and was now a prominent judge. To protect her, he had to get to the bottom of why she was being attacked. While he would have to think of himself later, she did say that she thought they were connected. Exactly what did she mean? He had to know.

## Chapter 14

After making the margarita, Noella settled into the couch. It felt funny that he wasn't pursuing her like most guys had in the past. She remembered the last guy, the one who'd turned into a giant leach when she was finally alone with him. It took a while to make him finally understand what *no* meant. While she had been ready that night for some fun, she simply didn't want to be used as a piece of meat. That would never happen.

What was it about Vance that made her shift into an aggressive mode? Was this turning him off? She assumed she still looked sexy.

She adjusted the pillow on the couch, and tasted the drink she had made. Not bad. The rush of heat soon soothed her mind. Her nerves had held up nicely until now, but how much longer would they serve her?

She felt the signature motion of the boat shifting slightly. It had to be Vance coming aboard. Snuggling in his arms again tonight would be fantastic. Getting used to not having him around later would be hard, but she had managed on her own for a while now.

What was taking him so long? She felt no more shifts in the boat, as she patiently waited and waited. She decided to stand and venture toward the front of the boat. "Vance, are you here?"

No answer. Where was the pistol? Did he leave it for her this time? She glanced around, but saw nothing she could use as a weapon. Her heart pounded. She opened a drawer, and found a knife. Now what?

Again, she waited for what seemed like forever, but still no response. "Vance?" Finally, she felt another slight shift in the boat as an image of a person drifted across the front of the boat. Could it be Vance? Whoever it was quickly moved closer to the door and stopped. When the door opened, she felt the immediate relief of Vance smiling at her.

"Damn, you keep scaring me!" She rushed into his arms.

With a curious smile, he answered, "Why?"

"You didn't answer my call to you."

"What call?"

"The one when you first came on board several

minutes ago."

"I never heard you, and I've just now returned."

"It was about five to ten minutes ago."

She watched the seriousness of the words reflect on his face. "Stay here. I'll be right back."

"Hell no! I'm staying right with you." She raised her knife to reveal her only weapon.

"Okay, but stay close to me." He raised a gun as she had thoughts from a movie where the bad guy said something like bringing a knife to a gun fight. Whatever. It did make her feel slightly safer in holding on to it.

She stayed close to him as he walked out the door. He stopped, and looked both ways. While the harbor was quiet and relaxing for some, it felt eerie for her. While she had been here before only a few times, she had never seen it so deserted.

After several minutes of studying the marina, she still saw nothing. Suddenly she watched Vance concentrating on a boat docked across from them. "Do you recognize that boat, Noella?"

"No, but that means nothing to me. I don't come here that often."

"For some reason, I think they're watching us."
He lowered his head and pulled her behind him. "I
need some of my equipment."

Minutes later, she watched him switch off his
iPod. "I think we're safe for now, but if I were to
guess, we had a tracking device added to the side of
the boat."

"Really?"

"Yes. I'm sure the FBI has wasted no time in
figuring out where you had vanished to."

"The FBI would be much better than my attacker,
but how can you be sure?"

"They're the only one capable of such
sophisticated surveillance. I think I saw night vision
goggles on a guy across the bay, and it would take a
frog man to plant a bug below the water line on this
boat."

"How did you learn all of this?"

"I've had plenty of time on my hands lately." He
turned to face her. "I guess one thing is good out of all
of this. Unless the guy who is behind attacking you is
connected with the FBI, we're going to be very safe
tonight."

She watched him write a note. "We might be heard talking. So for their benefit, let's pretend to be going to bed and with you in one stateroom and me in another. I'll have the problem corrected by tomorrow."

Noella reached over and scribbled, "Okay. But can we whisper?"

"Yes," he whispered softly. "But first, let us make them think they have the rest of the night off."

Noella winked and raised the sound of her voice. "I think this drink is all I need to sleep tonight. You can stay up late tonight if you want, but I'm going to bed. You should find everything you need in your stateroom."

"Sleep tight. I need to do some research. Thank you for the use of the guest stateroom." Vance nodded like that should do it, but then added, "You don't mind if I listen to some music, do you?"

"No, not at all. It is piped throughout the boat, but I can turn it off in my stateroom."

"Good."

She watched Vance turn the music on before he reached for his backpack he had with him. For several minutes she watched him assemble some kind of electronic device. After offering a smile, he walked over and turned the radio louder. Finally, he leaned forward and whispered, "Do you have any idea why the FBI wants to track you?"

"None, but I think I can find out by asking them tomorrow."

"No. Let's keep this quiet for now. We might be able to take advantage of this by feeding them some information."

"Do you care to let me in on this?"

"After seeing the detective's car show up tonight, we both know someone inside the force is not going to be happy. It would be great if the FBI made the case on their own. I just need to find out what info to feed them."

"This sounds like a job internal affairs should handle."

"And what makes you think someone in internal affairs isn't involved?"

"I see your point."

She watched him drink his margarita in one long gulp. "The detective we videoed must have known he might be watched since he left immediately. I wish we could have identified him."

"So what is our next move?"

"I'm going to the prison to try to see Xavier and cash in one of our chips. If he thinks I'm not going to be a threat to him, and that I might also want to extract some mutual revenge, he might open to me. We'll see."

"If I'm going to be any good tomorrow in the court, I also need some sleep. I promise I won't seduce you tonight." She had to smile slightly, as she remembered the previous night. "I'll have to admit that I'm getting used to you being in bed with me."

"I think we both know it's mutual." Vance stood to turn off lights and usher her along to the stateroom. As soon as he began to strip, her heart quickly started to beat faster. Yes she was watching him. He was hot. She thought about matching his disrobing speed, but stopped.

Cold water on her face is what she really needed. She found her nightshirt and walked into the bathroom. She forced herself to slow down, to breathe easier. Tonight would be one of only cuddling, and sleeping. Minutes later, she had stripped, and slipped into the night clothes. She opened the door slightly, and saw his back. Was he already asleep?

As she stepped forward, the floor creaked and he turned onto his back with his eyes wide open. With mixed feelings, she turned off the light on the table and edged over closer to him. As she suspected, he was sleeping totally nude again. This time, he was the one who wasn't playing fair.

She soon felt a warm kiss on her forehead. "I always thought I would love to live on a boat. This only makes the desire bigger."

What she had always really wanted was a guy who loved her both in and out of the bed. The bed could be anywhere. "Vance, what are we doing? We have to talk about our future at some point," she whispered.

"I agree, but we have so much to talk about. The most important thing for me right now is keeping you safe, and the best way to do that is to find out why you're being attacked."

Noella wanted to blurt it out. She wanted to know why he really left her years ago. She wasn't ready for it to be over then, or for it to end again. What was he hiding?

### 

Vance knew he had to put an end to this. There was no way a long term relationship could be built with Noella. She was a prominent judge, and he was a guy who got kicked off the police force, and reduced to doing odd bodyguard jobs.

It felt so strange that her father had stayed away from her during all of this. He was also the one guy who held answers to his father's suicide, and to why his father had gambled his fortune away.

Vance also knew that he was part of the scandal his father was accused of. If he had pushed the facts he knew, it would have damaged Noella's father's reputation, and thus also Noella. He couldn't let that happen. The main internal conflict he had struggled with since his dad's death concerned his mother. She had deserved so much better than what she had received.

As he had done for the last seven years, he tried to push the thoughts out of his head. Had it been long enough to forget the past, and make a new start?

## Chapter 15

After Vance dropped Noella off at the courthouse and made sure she made it safely inside, the kiss he had received moments earlier still lingered on his lips. He was slipping into a life he had no way of maintaining. Why did he do this to himself? He needed to find a solution. Today he hoped to find some answers, and was prepared for all kind of contingencies.

He knew he was going to be watched since the local police station and the Feds had an interest in following his activities. After last night, the gang leaders would also know that he was on the case. Without a doubt, he knew that the person responsible for the attacks had to be taking notice. After all, he had killed several of their people. He could only imagine what kind of revenge they had planned for him later.

While the chances of finding out who had set him up and had him dismissed from the force might be hidden forever, he hoped to push the envelope on it while he had the chance. He knew of no reasons to be subtle now.

Since he knew that he would be searched as he entered the prison, he had made previous plans to leave all weapons and electronics safely stored. As he assumed, the officer at the front desk appeared to be tipped off that he was coming. "You need to have a seat. The warden wants to talk to you first."

The warden! Yes, he definitely had someone's attention. He acted surprise, but he'd kind of expected this. "How long will this take? I kind of need to get back to Tampa soon."

"Not long. He wants to make sure you understand some rules here."

True to his words, the warden walked in to greet him. "Hello, Vance. I've . . . as you can imagine, been told that you'd show up here soon. Xavier has an attorney and usually never talks to anyone unless his lawyer is present."

"I can understand, and I do appreciate that, but if I can get a message to him I would appreciate it very much."

The Warden hesitated as he studied him. "Why is

it so important that you talk to him?"

"I'm just looking for the truth." Vance leaned closer. "Let's just say I saw some friends of his in Ybor City last night who wanted me to check on him."

"I don't think he'll be impressed by that enough to see you."

"They didn't think so either, since they have decided to make some new friends. Just tell him that I'm no *black knight* trying to destroy the world. If anything, some people think I'm simply a guy on the *sidelines*. I'm off the force now. I just thought it would be good to put closure to a few things while I had the chance."

Vance watched the keywords register in his dilated eyes. "I can send him the request. It's up to him if he wants to see you." While the warden struggled to maintain a straight face, Vance knew he had his attention.

"I understand, but can't wait all day. I just thought he might like some company after being in here for a while." Vance knew the coded words would be sent.

The warden stood and walked out. Fifteen minutes later, he returned. "They're getting him ready for you now." He focused on Vance intensely before he continued. "You'll be talking through a glass. Sorry, but this is necessary, and just remember that everything you say and do will be recorded."

"I wouldn't expect anything less."

Minutes later, Vance watched Xavier being directed to a table in front of him. He appeared very different from the last time he had seen him. His hair had been cut and he had shaved off his beard. Vance realized that since he was preparing for a retrial, the attorney had been prepping him well. For this last year, he was also off drugs and perhaps thinking straight.

However, as Xavier came closer, the deadly intensity of his focus centered in on Vance. "I heard you wanted to see me."

"I thought it might be good for us to talk." Vance glanced to his side where a uniformed officer stayed close. He then studied the video camera focused on him. What he had to do was delicate.

"I'm listening." Trust was going to be hard, and he had no intentions of making it any easier.

"I heard your case is being heard and that it might

be remanded back to a lower court."

"On that question . . . you'll have to ask my attorney." Xavier raised his shackled hands to make a point. "They tell me very little inside here."

"I can understand. What you might not know is that the judge who sent you here is being attacked by someone."

"Really, and you think I'm responsible while I sit here and rot."

"Not exactly. And I do not mean to imply that there is a connection."

"Then what in the fuck are you doing here?"

"Making conversation. For what it is worth, I don't think I'm the one who shot any *innocent* women the day the sting went down." Vance leaned closer to the glass. "I'd like to offer my deepest apology for any involvement I had." Vance knew that Xavier had a relationship with one of the women, but had hidden the information until now.

Xavier appeared to soften, as he seemed to understand. "They were here trying to start over and enjoy the American life—some life."

"Yeah, tell me about it."

"There are many people like them out on the street."

"Yes, and it's going to be bad, with so many people on the take, and you know, like cashing in on them." Okay, this was about as close as he could get to learning what he wanted to know. Would he talk now?

"The street always has a way of taking care of its own."

"True. That is when it's left alone. We both know there are good knights out there, and black evil ones."

Xavier tapped his fingers on the table in front of him. This might be the best way Xavier had to respond that he understood. Vance knew the code. One tap is a *yes,* and two taps was a *no*. Did anyone here know it? He decided to push and find out later.

"Being in here, I assume you might not have heard about the attacks on the judge."

Xavier kept a plain face, but his fingers tapped once. Okay, so he knew something.

"We both know that I would love to find out who is behind the attacks on the judge."

"I know nothing."

"I understand, but we both know that if your case

is remanded to her, she would probably rule the same way as before."

"Not necessarily. Certain information this time might not be allowed." So Xavier knew about the case, and what the game plan was.

Xavier leaned closer to the glass. "Here is one thing for you to think about. If it appears that I'm threatening the judge, the chances of being remanded are going to be harder to obtain. Just saying."

This did make sense. But in this case, it had to be someone who wanted to make sure he was not released. The person who first came to mind would be the new leader of the gang. Should he push? Hell yes!

"As you probably know, I've always thought I had been set up."

"Welcome to the club."

"And we might be facing a common enemy—yes?"

While Xavier's laugh was full of a sinister overtone, it edged on a strange sense of comradery. "That would be a real shitter, now wouldn't it?"

"I know you were given several chances to turn state evidence, but you decided to not do so. I guess

I'd never get a straight answer on that, would I?"

Vance watched two finger taps on the table. "I was accused of some very bad crimes. Trying to survive on the street is not as easy as you white boys think." Xavier offered an ever so slight wink—a coded message of some kind.

"If you think you were set up, why didn't you work on that angle when you were being prosecuted?"

No reaction.

"I know it's hard to know who your friends and enemies are at times." Now was the time. "Do you think it was someone who worked with you that turned against you?"

Vance watched a clear, but undeniable, single tap on the table.

"There was also speculation that someone on the force was helping you protect the illegal workers you found jobs for."

He tapped one time again, indicating that he had inside help from the police force. "I think there's nothing wrong with finding jobs for friends, is there?"

"I think we both know the charges were for extorting money from the employers."

"Yes. That's what they alleged. It's interesting that the people who hired the workers never do a day in jail."

"Are you referring to Pedro?"

"No, not to any one person in particular." However, his finger tapped once.

Vance had a clear idea who needed to be investigated. He also had discovered a new reason for the case not to be remanded. If freed, it would mean that Xavier would take over his old job again and thus ending Pedro's new job. Proving this would be hard, especially without much help from inside the force.

He now needed one name: the person responsible for framing him, and for eliminating Xavier from the equation. He knew more than ever that it had to be a cop on the inside, and someone working the gangs like he had. Still, there were many officers on these special tasks force.

"I think I have answered many questions for you, and perhaps too many." Xavier paused. "You know that detective Nelson came by earlier, asking me these same questions."

"Nelson. I didn't know he was involved in this

case."

"I guess when you got canned they had to reassign it to someone."

Yes it made sense to some extent, but what kind of message was he trying to send to him. Was Nelson involved with this more than he knew?

"I see. Maybe I need to touch base with him."

Vance watched a single tap.

"I'm sure he'll tell me everything. He always was someone I could trust."

Then, the unexpected—two taps. Now he knew, but could this be true?

## Chapter 16

Noella knew the chances of Vance learning anything were highly unlikely, but she didn't need him to be underfoot during the day. The FBI agents would be there soon to talk to her and bring her up to date. She was ready for this to be over.

While she was waiting, her phone rang. "Hello, honey. I had a few minutes, and wanted to check on you."

"Thanks, dad. I've been wanting to call you, but . . . well you know how it's been."

"I only know what I see in the news. However, I heard that Vance is now providing bodyguard services for you. How did that happen? I thought you two were finished years ago."

"As you know, we broke up when his father died. Life hasn't been easy for him since then. But for now, he has saved my life several times. I know you're afraid he'll hurt me again, but it's different this time."

"His dad caused a major scandal for the law firm

when he committed suicide. I don't think we'll ever know all of the reasons behind what happened. No one would have ever thought he would gamble away all of his money. Has Vance said anything about this to you?"

"No, he never discusses his past at all. While I would love for him to talk to me and learn what really happened to us, I don't think that will ever happen."

Her dad paused before his voice deepened, representing a sign of major concern. "You might not like what you find out."

"Why is that?" Now, she knew her dad had more information she needed.

"There's almost always more to the story than what most people want to know."

"I understand, but I would love for him to talk to me." Noella wondered if she would ever know the truth. "I'll talk to you later, dad."

A barrage of thoughts crossed her mind as she waited for the FBI agents. What was the real reason her father called, and what else did he know that he was not telling her?

Soon, the agents walked in to see her. "Hello,

gentlemen. I hope you have some good news for me.”

“Not really, but we need your help.”

“How is that?”

“Vance is digging into an area where he doesn’t know what he’s doing. He’s about to blow an investigation we have in place.”

Interesting. Noella knew Vance was asking questions at the prison. Apparently he was stepping on some toes. “Since we’re talking about threats to my life, do you want to tell me something I need to know?”

“We know that there has been money offered to intimidate you and to make such well known. If they really wanted to take you out, it would be much lower key. This has been confusing to us. We now have a hunch why that is.”

“And?”

“There is a strong possibility that a case might be remanded back to you. I think you know the one we’re talking about. If it comes with new instructions on how to conduct the case, it’ll make a difference in one person being convicted or not. We now think there are people who don’t want him back.”

While she agreed with the comments, she waited on more information without acknowledging them. "Interesting. Go on."

"We don't know who the main player in all of this is, but we know some of the small players. Vance is causing problems that he doesn't understand. This investigation will come to an end soon and we would really like for you to trust us with your protection until then."

"I think you're already providing with me with protection."

"What do you mean?" His eye brow arched as he also lifted his head.

"Come on. We both know you're keeping me under twenty four hour surveillance." She felt like he was lying, but wanted to leave the conversation in place, just in case he had more to add.

"We would love to, but Vance has made it hard to know where you are."

Noella had to think fast and decide what to divulge. "Are you telling me you're not watching me?"

The FBI agent looked stunned. "What exactly are

you asking?"

She needed to stall until she talked to Vance again. "Nothing, I think we have a breakdown in communications. What I need to know is how much longer this will take?"

"Maybe a week. Perhaps it would be a good time for you to take a vacation somewhere."

"Not in my plans. I've also made it clear that I don't trust the Tampa police. Maybe I said that wrong. I still think there is someone in the Tampa police department connected with this. Is there anything there you can share with me?"

"We're doing a full investigation and we're also working with the Tampa internal affairs department. While it would be improper for us to disclose anything we suspect at this time, we will when the time is right. However, I will say that we don't suspect that the threats are coming directly from them."

"I hope you're right."

"For now, will you tell Vance to cool it and not compromise our investigation?"

"His main job is to keep me safe. I'll only tell him what I feel he needs to know to do his job. I want this over with as soon as possible like everyone else."

"Let us know if you change your mind about the protection. It's still available for you."

Noella watched the men leave, knowing they were keeping several cards hidden from her. What in the hell had Vance found out?

## Chapter 17

Vance escorted Noella onto the boat, which was quickly feeling like home. "I did some quick shopping today and I hope to prepare something nice for us tonight."

"Thanks, I'm hungry. However, what I really want to know is what you found out today. Also, the people onboard the boat that you think might be watching us are not part of the FBI."

"How do you know that?" This was a game changer, and he prepared to move fast.

"They don't know where I am. I'm sure of it."

"I see." He leaned forward to whisper. "In such a case, someone else might be listening to us. I'll be back in a minute."

Vance grabbed his backpack and eased toward the door. He stopped briefly to turn on the music.

Outside, he moved quickly along the pier. The boat across from them had disappeared. If it wasn't the FBI, who was it? Someone knew they were there and they were apparently content to silently wait until now. Since he wasn't sure if they were safe or not, he had to make a move quickly before they knew what was happening.

He knew that removing her from the boat now would make her an open target. As he hurried back to the boat, he thought that their best chance of survival was to make a run for it in the boat.

The music was playing loud as he entered the boat. He whispered, "We need to make a run for it. Keep your head down and I'll get us moving as quickly as I can."

"I can help."

"Trust me. I need you to stay down. I'll let you know what you can do." Vance grabbed two bullet proof vests and handed one to her.

He watched her shake. "Perhaps we should call the police."

"Someone in the police department may be behind this. No! We need to make a run for it tonight, and I'll make some better inroads tomorrow into who is behind this. I have a suspicion as to who it is."

Vance quickly slipped outside and untied the

lines. Moments later he fired up the engines. Since he knew they would be after him in minutes, the normal warming up time had to be shortened. To hell with the motors for now he thought as he turned to Noella. "Let's do it."

Within minutes he eased the yacht out of the slip and into the harbor. Suddenly he heard a bullet whiz by his head, striking the boat. Like it or not, he needed back up. While staying low, he made it to the lower bridge and forced Noella to the floor. "Call the Coast Guard, we're being shot at."

"What?"

"Just do it!"

Vance peered over the top of the deck. He saw no one, but they could be following in the dark. He went full throttle, hoping to put some space between them.

He heard Noella yell. "They want to know where we're heading and they'll try to catch up with us. They also will have a copter in the air in a minute."

"Good. Tell them we're heading out toward the gulf and that we'll signal them when we see them."

Ten minutes later he saw a flashing light racing after them. Vance lowered the speed and waited for them to catch up. Flood lights soon overpowered his vision with an officer boarding the boat minutes later. "Are you okay?"

"Yes, but we just had another attempt on the judge and I need to get her somewhere safe"

"Understood. Do you want us to provide transportation or escort you somewhere?"

"I think someone knows this boat is where we are so it'll be useless. We need to return it to Clearwater. I'll arrange transportation for us when we get there."

"Very good." The officer hesitated as he pointed toward the cabin. "If there's a bullet lodged there we'll need to treat this boat as a crime scene."

"Understood. Has the marina been locked down? The shooter may still be there."

"The Tampa police are doing their job there now."

Vance knew what kind of help he would receive in learning anything from them. "Good." He felt like the Coast Guard could be trusted, but he had no reason to tell them what he thought of the Tampa police force.

The officer waved out toward the gulf. "We'll follow you to Clearwater, if that's where you want to go. I assume you would want an escort."

"Yes, that would be nice. Thanks."

###

Noella felt her heart beating. Another attempt on her life, and this time, they had fired at Vance. Enough was enough. Tomorrow she would demand full protection. She wanted Vance to stay beside her, but she also wanted the FBI to do their job until this was over. She quickly wondered what plans Vance had for the rest of the night to keep her safe.

She watched him return to the helm as he answered her unspoken questions. "We need to run at full speed and return the boat. I'll have a rental car there waiting on us."

"Where are we going?"

"Somewhere not nearly so obvious. Tomorrow we'll make another move. I hate to say it, but a hotel next to the court with full FBI coverage might be the best solution."

"I was thinking the same thing, but it will mean not sleeping with you again."

"Unfortunately . . . yes." He leaned over and kissed her forehead. "As I've said before, after all of this is over we'll talk. Deal?"

She felt relieved as she whispered, "I would like that."

She soon helped him to navigate the narrow harbor in Clearwater. After quickly securing the boat, she watched Vance pull a light jacket from her dad's closet. "Is it okay if I borrow this?"

"Sure." She wanted to laugh at the word borrow, but didn't.

"I know a cheap motel close to here, and one where no one will ask questions. Tomorrow we'll check you into a nice place closer to the courthouse."

"Good." She knew they would have this one last night together. She had to make the most of it. She didn't know if she was scared of being attacked again, or scared of losing him after the night.

Vance pulled quickly into a small motel. He wasn't kidding. After a quick sign in, he rushed back to the car and helped her to a room. We won't be here long. After we get you settled into a better hotel tomorrow, I'll be glad to go to your house and retrieve some clothes for you."

"We can both go after work. I'm sure we'll have a police escort everywhere from now on."

"Yes. We need to get to the bottom of this quickly."

"Since we won't have much time to talk after tomorrow, I need to know everything you found out today."

"I was warned to not trust the person that was going to be my partner on the force. While this is hard to believe, I'll have to check it out."

"What else?"

"I need to see who is taking over for Xavier. I don't think he was the main man in the operations he was sent to prison for. He may have been simply a front man."

"I saw the evidence on him, and it was more than persuasive."

"I'm sure it was, but it could have been planted. Both of us could have been played." Vance tightened his fist at the thought of being manipulated.

"He had every chance to cooperate with law officials, but decided to not do so. However, since you did the investigation on him, you have to know much more than I do."

"I learned a lot about him, and how he works. He

was an opportunist, but he also cared for the people he helped to find jobs for." Vance tried to compare what he knew with what he suspected. He needed to get back into the records at the police station. The bullet tonight was not targeted for the judge. Someone had taken a shot at him. Okay, so he meant to rattle some cages today with his visit to Xavier, but damn, word traveled fast.

The inside of the hotel room looked plain and simple. He could relax here, but he knew it was much lower in standards than Noella had ever accepted. It would just be the one night, and then she would be in one of the best hotels in Tampa.

It dawned on him that tonight might be the last night with her. Was the last few nights all about sex, or was there an old flame there that could develop into something more?

As he waited for Noella to check out the room, his mind refocused on the time seven years ago when he decided to call it quits. He had spent a week going over the details of his dad's betting. He almost never won. He always had to send more money to cover his losses.

But even if he was totally broke and embarrassed, he was still a damn good lawyer with a future. The partnership agreement on selling his interest of the firm hadn't been updated for years, which effectively left little money to go to him and his mother. He knew his father's death was an embarrassment to the firm, and they wanted it to disappear as fast as possible. Word had been circulated that he might have taken some client's money and used it to cover his bets. While this was never proven, and since there was no money to go after, all suits were quickly dropped. However, the scandal had been created, one which still lived in many people's minds.

It was the words of Noella's father which finally made him realize that he had to move on. While Vance's father had no money for anyone to go after, the firm did. So while his life of luxury was over, Vance saw no reason to destroy Noella's also. He had always loved her and wanted the best for her. While he knew Noella's father had made some maneuvers to protect the firm, some of his actions might have hidden what really happened. Hush money had to be involved. For this, Vance held him responsible, but going after him with a law suit would only ruin Noella.

The conflict between being loyal to his mom and to Noella had torn him apart for years. After he had finally made peace with himself, this happened to bring it all back to the present. He had to now decide if he could truly put it in the past and keep it hidden from everyone. Noella's father would be the key. In order to move forward, he knew that he had to know what was hidden from him.

As if waking from a daze, he focused on Noella's smile, as she jokingly observed. "Perhaps it looks better in dim light."

He was too tired to laugh. "We both need some sleep. We both have big days ahead of us."

"Do you think they'll ever find out who shot at us tonight?"

"I doubt it. Tomorrow, I need to get some answers." He knew exactly where to start.

"How do you plan on doing that?"

"I'm going to see who is taking over for Xavier, and find out who is the real person in charge."

She acted protectively. "As much as you hate to

acknowledge it, you might need protection also."

"Funny, but true." Vance started to take off the jacket he had borrowed from her dad. It felt funny they were about the same size. Out of habit he reached into the pockets to empty everything as he prepared to take it off. After he felt some papers in the bottom of one of them he decided to wait for a minute. Whatever they were, they were not his.

Noella glanced at the bathroom. "I think it would be good to have a quick shower before I go to bed."

"I understand. Help yourself while I'll make sure all is quiet outside." Curiosity had his mind working on what papers he had in his pocket. Yes, he was nosey.

"I'll not be long." She leaned over and kissed his lips softly before she turned and walked to the bathroom. Her ass looked great. Sex would be good tonight. He highly suspected that might happen again.

After the door closed, he retrieved the papers and opened them where he could read. He saw copies of deposit slips to a bank he recognized. This was the one his dad had to send money to cover his betting losses. There was also another bank name he didn't recognize.

Her dad was more involved in this than he thought. He also saw two account numbers. Damn! This just might be a way to track down who these operators were who took his father's money. While he had placed this out of his mind earlier, he needed to reopen it soon. He quickly placed the papers in his backpack so that he could study them in more detail later.

He heard the water running, which reminded him that he also needed a shower. Since it might be their last night together, he might as well make the most of it. Some bodyguard he had turned out to be. He quickly dropped the coat on the chest along with the t-shirt that he pulled over his head. The pants and boxers soon followed.

After he opened the door, which naturally was not locked, he saw her naked body shimmering through the thin shower curtain. When he pulled the curtain to the side, he watched her smile.

"I was hoping you'd join me." She reached for his hand to guide him closer to her. Her breasts looked full and plump, with the nipples slightly excited and pink.

"I saw no reason in wasting perfectly hot water." He stopped talking and wrapped his arms around her before pulling her closer to him, where she appeared to melt into his body. Her firm body had a softness he loved.

She stood on her tiptoes, and stretched for his lips. He accommodated her and kissed her lips with immediate passion, as he pushed hard against her. She quickly opened her mouth and begged for French style kissing.

He turned her sideways where the hot water would bathe both of them. His hand moved to one of her breast, where he started to explore and caress the texture of her skin. Her nipple responded by hardening more, as she added a small moan.

After sliding his free hand lower, he studied the way she was trimmed, but not shaved. To him this was perfect. He quickly slipped lower and studied her folds. She appeared to be ready. Should he take her in the shower? They, after all, had all night to make love in the bed.

When she wrapped her fingers around his manhood, he knew the answer. Minutes later, she wrapped her arms around his neck as he lifted her off the ground. He felt her legs spread and lift higher as they worked around his butt. He slipped inside with ease. It was as if they had been a couple for a long time.

He entered and pulled out of her with ease. While each motion felt better than the previous, this slow rate could help him last all night. Eventually she appeared to understand. "I guess we need to move it to the bed."

"That would be nice." He reached behind him and turned off the water. The instant cold air hit him. "Let me find us a towel."

After stepping out of the shower, he almost laughed. Instead of the large luxurious towels she was used to, these little napkins would not do much good. Since that was all they had, he offered her both towels. "Here, you need to dry and not catch a cold."

After drying the best they could, they walked to the bed, her every movement exciting him more. She apparently didn't mind him seeing her naked and she did have a great looking butt. When she turned, he could see everything, since it was barely hidden by the small patch of black hairs.

She quickly came closer and snuggled next to him by resting on his shoulder. "Vance, make me one promise."

He hesitated. "Maybe."

"Promise me that when this is all over you'll talk to me about what happened to us when we dated earlier."

"Are you sure you want to go there?"

"I think we need to if we're going to move forward. I wasn't ready for it to end then, and I'm not ready for it to end now."

"Sometimes actions you might take as unloving are really the ultimate in love. I'll explain that one day. We need to see how all of this plays out. Okay?"

"Whatever it is that might be holding us apart, I promise I can handle it." Her voice quivered, as she breathed in deeply.

"I wish life was that simple. However, I might be able to resolve some questions I have soon." He wished he could offer her more hope, but he still had many unknown pieces that he needed to fit together.

### 

As soon as he parked his truck, Vance knew his life was going to change fast. While he felt like he could trust the FBI now, it was his friends that he thought he'd had in the Tampa police force that were now very questionable.

He quickly thought about the warning he had received earlier. It wasn't about certain officers that he had suspected, but the guy who was to be his partner. Thinking about him, he didn't know that much— really. That would all change soon.

The two FBI officers he recognized from earlier greeted him as he walked into the lobby. "We're so glad you finally decided to trust us. We found a bullet in the side of the hull of your dad's boat this morning."

Vance stepped forward. "I'll still be available for any personal trips she wants me to accompany her on. I don't guess you have any leads on who is behind this that you can share."

"I'm sure you realize how much we have to guard what we know."

"Yeah, I thought so. However, I might have more information for you soon. I can't say anything right now either, but the person we might be after is totally off the radar." Vance knew that would totally get their interest.

"We would love to hear what you think."

"Later tonight, I think we might need to talk. Give me until then."

He watched Noella listening to every word. He didn't really want her to question why he wasn't confiding in her. If he was lucky, he could find answers to many questions, and maybe even set the stage for a life with her. Maybe it was only the slight promise of a dream, but one worth pursuing.

Before he could be pressured into telling more, Vance turned and left. He needed to return to the police station to find answers.

Twenty minutes later, he walked through the front door of the police station, and toward the same officer who was reprimanded earlier. "Good morning. I'm going to need a room and access to the files again. I also want to have Nelson accompany me."

With a forced smile, the officer responded, "I'll see if he's available."

Offering an intent stare as he waited, Vance made it clear he had no time to waste. He stepped toward the hallway leading to the room that he occupied before.

"I'll have to check you for weapons first."

"No problem." The only weapon he had was a

flash drive he planned to use to store information. Assuming that Xavier was right, he planned to keep Nelson in sight until this was over.

Once inside the small office, Vance went to work. He first accessed anything related to the Xavier case being remanded back to Noella. He tried to hide the fact that he was more interested in who else was following the developments of this case. Naturally, many people had checked into the data file, but the one name he saw the most was that of Nelson. Yes, this was a case he would have interest in, but what kind of interest was now the question. He decided to follow the trail of what all he had searched. It was not long until he saw the code word *black knight*. He needed to know more about it, and who was in charge of it. The answer shocked him, but confirmed what he was told by Xavier. Nelson was heavily involved in the investigation.

Since Nelson would be there soon, he slipped in the flash drive and quickly downloaded what he needed. He would have more time to analyze his findings later.

Nelson eventually walked in. "I was told to come

see you.”

“Hey, buddy.” Vance decided to act friendly and keep his suspicions to himself for as long as he could. “I need your help. As I’m sure you have already heard, I went to see Xavier yesterday. While it was much as I suspected—a wasted trip, I want to check on some things and I hope you can go with me. I’m sure we can clear this with the chief if you wish. The judge is wanting answers fast.”

“Vance, I heard you were shot at again last night. Damn it! This might be a good time for you to let us take care of doing the investigation. Hey, man, you know I have your best interest here, and I’ll tell you everything I can find out.”

Sure he would. While Nelson sounded sincere, Vance studied his eyes, and knew that he was lying or hiding something important. “Nelson, you know there’s no way I’ll walk away from this. I want to go see Pedro Sanchez.” Vance studied the slight twitch in his facial muscles. He had hit a nerve.

“Pedro was nearly put out of business by Xavier, and we both know that he was being extorted for a huge amount of money that Xavier used to fund his own operations."

"Funny. Of all of these funds Xavier was supposedly making, no money of any amount was ever located. In fact, he had to use a public defender to represent him."

"That does not mean he doesn't have it stashed away somewhere for when he gets out." Nelson had lost all credibility as he tried to sideline him.

"That could be true. If he has his case sent back to Noella, there's no way of knowing how it will be decided this time, and the one person who will have an interest in the outcome of this retrial would have to be Pedro."

"Between you and me, he's being watched carefully by me and others. While he hires a lot of people in his construction business, it's through many subsidiary companies. Like it, or not, he needs cheap labor and has no time to fully check, or even comply with, all legal regulations."

"So how does he get away with it?"

"He often pays his workers in cash since they don't have checking accounts, and usually only hires them for one project at a time. We've been trying to prove he's breaking the law, but he is always clean when we make the raids."

"So you think someone is tipping him off?" While this was a direct question, it was one that he knew Nelson would expect.

"Either that, or he has changed his ways, which may very well be the case."

While Nelson was trying to convince him that he was on top it, Vance tried hard to not tip his own hand. "Still, I want to go see him, and I want you to go with me."

"While he's always in his office in the mornings, we'll not get far in asking him many questions since he guards his privacy very much."

"Well, we'll see, let's go."

"I need to stop by my desk and check out first."

Vance pointed to the phone on the desk. "You can do that from here." He had no intentions of letting Nelson out of his sight until he saw Pedro.

"Yeah, I guess I could, but I do need to go pee before we go."

"Me too, the coffee here never gets any better, does it?" Vance stood and turned off the computer.

Once inside the restroom, Nelson pointed to a stall. "I won't be long."

"Nothing like being regular." Once he finished, Vance stuck a small mic under the cabinet next to the urinal. "I'll be waiting for you outside."

As Vance stepped from the restroom, he stuck a small receiver in his ear and waited. He soon heard Nelson talking on the phone. "Listen, and don't say a word. I have to come see you in a little while. Don't worry. I'm here to run interference. This will all be over soon."

Vance had no doubt what he was dealing with now. How this all happened, and why, would be answered later. He removed the ear plug and waited. He definitely knew who one of his enemies was now.

### 

Noella wanted to see her father, especially since she felt sure that he knew much more than he was telling. He had been one of the partners where Vance's father had also worked seven years ago.

After being escorted by the FBI, she walked into his office, and shut the door behind her. "Hello, dad."

How long had it been since she saw him face to

face? Perhaps close to a year. He looked older, and tired. While his office looked expensively decorated, he had stacks of files scattered everywhere.

He tossed his glasses on the desk and attempted a smile. "You look good."

"Considering what I've been through, I'll accept that as a compliment." She walked to a seat directly across the desk from him, and didn't wait to be invited to have a seat. "Dad, I'll get straight to the point. I know you're busy. You're always busy."

He shifted his weight to the back of the chair and entwined his fingers while placing them in his lap. "You know how it is—unfortunately, this is life."

"I want to talk about Vance. I also want to know what you know about his father. I understand you want to protect your firm, but I want the truth."

He cleared his throat. "His father committed suicide. Since I think the evidence was very strong on this, the chances of foul play were very remote. As far as motive, he had gambled away a fortune and was in debt to many people. In regards to the full extent of this, I'm sure we'll most likely never know, since I'm also sure the mafia, or some gambling gang was involved in some of his dealings."

"You know that about the gangs, or the mafia?"

"No, not really. That part is speculation, but highly assumed by most people. Since he had no assets, they would feel that it was best to move on quietly."

"Did anyone ever contact you regarding collection on his debt? I want the truth."

"His legitimate debtors were paid out of his settlement with the firm. The firm paid out a reasonable amount for his interest, which was outlined in the partnership agreement. Unfortunately, there was not much left to cover living expenses for Vance and his mother."

"We both know that destroyed his future. He dropped out of law school and out of my life too."

"Things happen, and I could say I'm sorry. The firm is doing extremely well now, as you know. If you want, I can cover his cost of going back to law school. Is that what this is all about?"

"It would have helped if you had offered to do so back when he was in law school."

"As much as you don't want to hear this, the firm

had to protect itself in all of this also. There was a lot of speculation in the media that his father had used client's money to cover his losses. Such a scandal would have ruined us. Any money given to him at that time would have looked very suspicious."

Noella decided to try another approach. "Since the places he gambled were online, and thus illegal, couldn't there have been some way of, at least, recouping some of his losses?"

"For the record, I hired a private detective to do that. After a year of digging, he discovered nothing."

"After all this time, why are you willing to help Vance now?"

"The statute of limitation on filing any claims against the firm has recently expired. I hope you won't announce this to anyone."

"I understand, but there has to be more. I wasn't ready for the relationship with Vance to end. I would have stood by him."

"I know that, and I think Vance also knows that. This scandal caused by his dad's death will be remembered for a long time. By disappearing, he saved you, and the firm his dad loved, a lot of problems." Her father smiled. "I may have gotten older over the last seven years, but at least a little wiser." He paused to change the tone of his voice. "Unfortunately, the problem now is the latest scandal, and one which he has brought on himself. It was determined that it was his gun that killed two innocent women who were being smuggled."

"First, let me remind you that the true identities of these women have never been ascertained. Second, Vance was discovered unconscious, and transferred to the hospital for several weeks."

"The case was made that he fell during the gunfight and hit his head. Internal affairs had also determined that it was his gun that had fired the shots."

"So you're not buying the fact he might have been framed."

"If I was his attorney, I would make that case."

"If it had ever gone to trial, you could have tried. However, it was ended by his agreeing to leave the force." She had to look away, since she may have made a big mistake.

"We all know you had a part in that."

"I know Vance blames me for this, but I thought I

was doing the best thing for him. I'm sure he'll never see it that way."

Her dad played with his glasses, as if to play the part of a devil's advocate. "As a point of discussion, why would anyone want to frame him?"

"We both know he was working on breaking a case on racketeering. When the case was tried, in my court for Christ's sake, his testimony was never entered. It almost set Xavier free."

"It may be best if I don't know all the details in the trial, but it would mean that it was someone in the force that set him up." Her dad leaned forward. "Internal affairs would be all over this, and they have turned up nothing that has been reported."

"It could be they know something, but also remained quiet in order to help the prosecution."

"That is a lot of accusations to make."

"And that is why I'm here." She leaned closer to her father and focused her stare, as she asked for the truth. "Is there anything else from the past you have not told me?"

## Chapter 18

Vance studied the outside of Pedro's office. The marble walls covering the exterior of his three story office building indicated just how profitable his operations had been.

The secretary at the front desk looked Latin, and was definitely attractive enough to work as a model. Her shiny, black hair, and her over whitened, but perfect teeth almost detracted him from her large breasts, which were partly exposed. Her cleavage definitely caught Nelson's attention.

Vance stepped to one side as Nelson flashed his badge. "We need to see Pedro for a minute." Vance doubted this show of importance was necessary, but played along. He already knew that Pedro had been warned. Vance also assumed that Nelson had been there many times before.

The receptionist turned in her chair, revealing a perfect view of her long legs, which were only covered by a short, black skirt. "Please follow me."

After walking down a long hallway, she stopped, and turned to a corner office. "This is Christina, Mr. Sanchez's personal secretary. She'll take care of you."

Christina looked more like a super model than the receptionist. Pedro sure had a thing about hiring beautiful girls to work for him. Vance knew he had to be paying them much more than he would normal girls who performed such task. "Can I ask what you want to see Mr. Sanchez about?"

Nelson turned to Vance, and allowed him to tell why. "My name is Vance Mills, and I'm sure he'll remember me. I talked to Xavier in prison yesterday and thought he might like to hear what I was told. But if he does not want to hear, that's fine." Vance turned to Nelson. "I guess we can go."

Nelson looked shocked. As Vance watched the exchange between him and the secretary, he recognized just how much Nelson had missed his calling as an actor.

The secretary quickly lifted the phone. "Mr. Sanchez, there is a Vance Mills here to see you." A long pause. "I think it might be good to see him. It sounds like he has some information you might want to hear." Christina glanced at Vance and smiled. "Yes, sir." Christina slowly replaced the receiver. "He said he would be right out."

The door behind her soon opened and Pedro walked out to meet them. For a guy of Mexican descent he was a large guy. He had done well for himself in America. Since the expensive suit he wore was not customary for many people in the construction business, he apparently was not the kind of contractor who got his hands dirty.

Vance extended his hand for a quick shake. "Thank you for seeing me on such short notice."

"I don't have much time, but please come back to my office." Vance noticed how he ignored Nelson. He assumed that they must have had many conversations in the past. While trying to hide that relationship, it only confirmed its existence.

"I understand, and this won't take but a minute." Vance walked into his office. The elaborate office did not look like that of a contractor, but one of a guy intent on impressing others. The cherry-wood desk glowed from the warm lighting coming from many occasional lamps in the room. The paintings on the walls were highlighted with their own distinctive lighting system.

"Would you like a cigar?"

"No, I don't smoke." Vance studied the two men before he started. "Yesterday I visited the guy who was found guilty of extorting you a year ago."

Pedro smirked as he turned to one side. "I try to not think too much about him anymore. I hope they keep him there for a long time."

"That is definitely understandable. As I'm sure you have heard, the judge who sentenced him to jail has been attacked several times. I'm working as her personal bodyguard now."

"Yes. I watch the news. What does this have to do with me?"

"Probably nothing. What I'm doing is checking on any cases that might be placed in front of her, and become the bases of these attacks." It was time to strike. "What do you know of Xavier's case being remanded to her for a new trial?"

"I don't think it will be, but if it is, it is?"

"Xavier has obtained new information that will be disclosed this time. It appears that he has a good chance of being found not guilty."

"What new information?"

"He would not say specifically, but indicated that you would know. That is why I'm here. Why would he say that?"

"I have no idea what it is, or why he thinks I would know, but we all know that he'll say, or do anything to get out of jail." Apparently, his temper was barely staying under control as he acted more agitated by the minute.

Now was the time to keep the pressure on. "What I'm trying to do is connect some dots, and attempt to find out who is behind the attempts on the judges life. I don't think he has contact with anyone who worked with him since he's under full security, but maybe you can help me with this."

He watched the intense stare of Pedro as he spoke. "With what?" he asked roughly.

"Has anyone else attempted to take over his operations?"

"No, all is going smooth now. Why do you ask?"

"I'm just trying to make connections. I would think that the only people he has contacts with now are people in the police force who are allowed to visit him. You know, there was some talk then of bad cops involved with helping him operate."

Pedro smiled. "If I remember correctly, I think I heard that was a position you pushed, but one that was never proven."

"True, but that's soon to be corrected. In a plea bargain that I think he's working on, he'll be naming names to save his rear."

"Really?"

One more push was all he needed to make him mad. He knew it. "I would hope you would like to cooperate with me to get to the truth. That is if you don't already know the truth."

Pedro pointed a finger at Vance. "You know, I think this conversation has gone far enough. I was the victim in this case, remember?"

"It was definitely painted that way. I don't want to take any more of your time." Vance glanced around the room. "It appears you're doing very well for yourself."

"Our operations have been successful lately."

"I wish other contractors shared your luck. I'll be

back later."

Pedro offered a sinister smile, as he stood. "You know, I've heard that you also have been fired from the force. The world is full of crazy people. Take care of yourself."

Vance knew that Pedro was connected in some fashion. However, he knew he wouldn't get any more information out of him now. "Thank you for your time, Mr. Sanchez."

Once back in the car, Vance turned to Nelson. "I know you're working these gangs around Ybor City. Someone had to step in and take over Xavier's operations. Do you care to give me some names?"

"The number of undocumented workers has decreased significantly since Xavier has gone to prison. The best guess is that without someone to find them work, they have moved on to other cities. Perhaps this is the wrong case to connect to the judge."

"Tell me the truth. We both know Pedro is getting rich off cheap Mexican labor."

Nelson hesitated, as he faked his response. "Over the last year he has worked hard with the department to make sure his employees are well documented. He knew he would be under the spotlight for a long time. I think you'll find him to be a fully upright citizen now."

"Most contractors I know are barely alive with this economy. How is he doing so well?"

"He works hard."

"Sure he does. I saw how much he likes to impress rather than work hard. I would love to take a look at his records."

"Good luck on getting a judge to sign a warrant to see them."

"I think I know one judge that might."

Vance noticed another jerk reaction in Nelson. "You might be right. So what is your next move?"

"I think it's time to go back to the streets. I think that is where I can find some truths."

"Or get yourself killed."

"This time I'll be ready. I have no intention of anyone blindsiding me again. But I know I will have to do this alone." Okay, this was the set up. He knew he would have full support. He just wanted to make sure as hell that Nelson didn't know it. Now, did Nelson buy it or not? Would he take the bait?

### ###

After making it back to his office, Vance studied his place. Had it been bugged while he was out trying to save the world? Since he knew they would be waiting for him, he needed to get some rest if he was to stay out most of the night in Ybor City.

However, he also had another problem he wanted to tackle. He looked at the notes he had lifted from the pocket of Noella's dad. He had tried often to find out exactly who his dad was placing his bets through. In addition to the name he recognized, he saw another corporate bank name. He went to work on the computer, and soon located the bank in Switzerland. Bingo. The bank also owned a company that his father wired the money to. With the security laws they were famous for, he could understand how laundering money there would be possible, but still, it was a step forward.

He needed to talk to Noella's father. What was his connection to this? He picked up the phone and decided to call Noella at the hotel. She should be there by now.

She answered immediately. "Hello, Vance. How

are you?"

"I'm fine. I'm getting some answers, but still looking for others. I'll be out all night, and I wanted to touch base with you first."

"Vance, I've found out some things today that I need to let you know about. I talked to my dad today. I'm not sure what you have heard, but he has some explaining to do to you."

"I see." Vance also had questions of his own. "Can you please set it up for after lunch tomorrow? I'll need to get some sleep after working tonight."

"You're not planning on doing something stupid tonight, are you?"

"I'm going to get some answers tonight, but I don't think I will be doing it stupidly either. I plan to have lots of back up."

"Back up?"

"Trust me for now, and I'll explain everything tomorrow. I won't be able to rest until I know you're safe, and right now we have a major threat against you and with me not far behind. You take care tonight." He paused. "You know I care deeply about you." That was about as close as he could say what he really felt.

Everything depended on how he handled the night.

"Vance, you know I care about your safety also. I fell for you a long time ago, and I never stopped."

"Sleep tight, beautiful." Vance hung up before he said words he wanted to reserve for later.

### 

Vance entered the back door of the mobile control center used by the FBI. "It's about time you learned to trust us." The agent motioned to a seat.

"I'm sure that after what I did earlier, I'll be a major target. On the street I'll be like poison, and I'm sure no one will really talk to me, but then again Xavier had a big network. It's hard to believe that it's all gone. Again, I may be the one person someone might want to talk to."

"We have a makeup artist coming. Making you look like a Mexican is going to be a little bit of a challenge. Exactly how good is your Spanish?"

"I had two intense years, thanks to the Tampa police before I left. This is not the first time I've had to go under cover."

The agent smiled. "We know. Due to the high profile status of this case, we were able to bring in a lot of outside assets, which we have hidden from the local police. Just remember, you may have only this one shot at proving your case of police corruption."

"Trust me, I don't like being used as bait on a daily basis. I want this over as much as anyone."

"You'll be wearing almost full body armor. I don't have to tell you that a shot to the head might prove to be fatal. Remember, we'll never be that far from you."

"Okay, let's do this."

### 

Vance headed for the first place he wanted to check out. He knew he might have to make several trips to various bars, but this one was where many Spanish speaking locals hung out.

Trying to look like a Mexican who was trying to look like an American was comical, but this was dead serious work. His Spanish was good, but not perfect. He knew to talk little, and sound drunk if he needed to.

After entering, he found a back table and waited for a waitress. When she came to see him, he spoke slowly, "Una Cerveza, por favor."

She smiled and turned away. When she returned,

he handed her a five. She made the change on the spot without really ever looking at him. Good. He was inside and could survey the place for a while.

He knew it would not be long before someone would decide to check him out. A small group of three guys soon ventured in, and grabbed a table next to his. He hoped the mic was strong enough for the FBI to hear their conversation. They were all looking for work, and apparently they were there to meet someone later. Vance felt lucky. This might be a fruitful night, and with the FBI to document it. He still needed to work his way up the ladder to see who was working the undocumented workers. Who had taken Xavier's job?

He soon heard them talking again. One was telling how they might have to relocate. The others did not care as long as they had work. When a tall, slim guy soon joined them, they lowered their voices to talk. Vance made sure his mic was pointed directly at them.

The new guy spoke in Spanish, and told them since they had no papers they would be moved to Miami. It would cost them money, but they would have work. One guy asked about working in Tampa.

The reply was immediate, "You can return after you obtain working papers. You can only work for Pedro when you're able to prove you're legal. We'll get the necessary documentation for you in time."

Vance now understood. Pedro was trafficking them to Miami, and probably making a fortune off them there, and finding cheap labor for himself later by promising to get them legal papers in due time. If it was true, he had not only taken over Xavier's job, he had expanded on it.

When they had made agreements, the guy stood to leave. It was time for him to follow this guy and start to work up the ladder. He heard a voice coming from his earplug as he walked out of the bar. "You do not have to get too close to this guy, we have him monitored."

Vance whispered back. "I'm sure he'll make many stops. Let me know when you can identify him."

"When you get a few blocks away we'll pick up the guys in the bar for questioning also."

"Good."

The scene repeated several more times over the next few hours. Either he had not been spotted, or this guy was playing it very cool. To work so openly, he had to have protection from someone.

This guy constantly sent text messages. Vance hoped the FBI could intercept them. On this last stop the guy moved faster than normal and quickly ducked down a backstreet. Vance followed, while speaking into his microphone. "I think he might be on to us."

"It appears so. Let us follow him, and we'll bring you back in on it soon. Find somewhere to disappear for a while."

"That's kind of hard, since I'm in the middle of this backstreet." Vance reached over and retrieved his Glock. He knew he was being set up.

A voice he recognized spoke from the shadows. "Hello, Vance. You could not leave it alone, could you?"

"Nelson. I assumed I would see you sometime tonight."

"You can drop the weapon. I don't want to shoot you."

Vance saw two other men appear on both sides of him. He was outnumbered, but he had help coming. He had to stall. "Since this might be my last stand, so to speak, can you answer one question for me?”

“Maybe. Let me guess. You want to know *why*.”

“I assume money has something to do with it. But I was thinking about the day I was knocked unconscious. You’re the one who found me. You were going to be my partner. Did you see who hit me, or was that you?”

Nelson sneered at him. “You know, at the time I felt bad for hurting you so bad, but now I wish I had made it more permanent. Sorry, but this was simply business. Xavier was getting to be a problem. When I shot the two women I originally hoped to pin it on him, but instead, it got blamed on you. I was hoping to plant your gun in his hand, but he slipped away instead. Because of this, his case does not need to be reheard, and this case reopened. With all of the publicity in these attacks on the judge, we think the case would not be remanded back to her court.”

Now Vance understood the plan. “So Pedro was not a victim, but he was a hidden kingpin.”

“So now you know. Too bad you’ll never be able to tell anyone.”

Suddenly, flood lights blasted from overhead.

Vance hit the ground as bullets stung the air above him. A voice boomed from the copter. "This is the FBI, drop your guns now."

"Instead of surrendering, Vance watched many shots fired at the copter above them. After taking one bullet in his chest, Vance returned fire from a gun he quickly retrieved from his ankle holster, taking down one of the guys. Even with the bullet proof vest, the shot he had caught hurt like hell. With no time to recover, Vance fired again and connected with another guy. He watched Nelson quickly drop his gun. Good, he would need him to talk.

An agent ran into the area to help secure it. This part was over, but the major case was far from it. Since Pedro had to know they would be coming after him next, Vance damn well wanted to be part of it. While he thought the FBI owed him that, he would see.

One of the FBI guys walked over to him. "Vance, the guy you were following has been apprehended. Are you okay?" He leaned over closer to examine him. "We also have people on the way to detain Pedro. We have it all on tape. This should be more than enough to clear your name."

"But do we have enough to put Pedro away?"

"That depends on how much everyone will cooperate with the investigation."

"I know we'll need that to prove he ordered the attacks on the judge. I want to be there when he's arrested."

"While you earned it, you have to stay in the background—understood?"

"Absolutely." Vance walked over to Nelson. "We both know you didn't operate alone. Who else in involved?"

"Fuck you, Vance. You'll have to ask my attorney."

"I think we both know what happens to cops who are sentenced to jail. If I were you, I wouldn't expect any kind of plea bargain."

Nelson's eyes showed the harsh reality of what was in store from him. "I'll have a good lawyer."

"Really! Don't count on Pedro's money to be there for you. It's now time for you to see what hell is like on the other side of the law, the one you placed me in, where everyone will be against you."

An ambulance approached the scene, as another

agent yelled. "You're too late, these two guys are dead." Okay, so he had more kills to deal with, but later.

A sedan sped into the back road, and an agent he recognized emerged. "Vance, I heard you wanted to be part of this arrest, and I would be honored if you would join me."

"Your damn right. I would love to." Vance jumped into the back seat, as the agent followed him. "I assume you've a warrant for his arrest."

"Signed, sealed and delivered. I suspect we might meet some resistance, but we're getting prepared for it. It's possible he'll try to make a run for Mexico, or to Miami where he has connections."

As they approached Pedro's compound, several copters appeared over head. Blue lights lit up the perimeters. If Pedro planned to fight, it would be fruitless. The best he could hope for was to stall and have time to destroy any incriminating documents.

However, the guards at the front gate quickly lowered their weapons. Several agents rushed forward and secured forward positions. An announcement quickly followed, "This is the FBI. To everyone inside the house, raise your hands and come out now."

Several tense minutes passed with no sign of life. Another agent joined them. "The guards just confirmed that he's inside."

An automatic weapon suddenly blasted bullets at them from the house, pinning everyone temporarily behind their cover. Moments later, the return fire from the FBI was intense. Suddenly it stopped. Was it over? Or were they reloading?

A slight movement on top of the roof caught Vance's attention. This position could expose many agents. He reached for his Glock and fired several blasts.

"What are you shooting at?"

The answer came as a man fell from the roof. Agents quickly moved in closer to secure the area. One yelled, "He's alive."

Seconds later, the door opened, and several men walked out with their hands in the air. One yelled in Spanish, "We're unarmed. We are innocent–please no shoot!"

Vance knew those facts would come out later. For now, they would be handcuffed and taken in for questioning. Where was Pedro?

As several agents stormed the house, Vance walked over to the guy he had shot on the roof. Pedro.

Pedro looked up at Vance with blood coming from his mouth as he spoke, "You sorry son of a bitch. We should have killed you earlier."

"We all make mistakes."

## Chapter 19

The FBI took most of the night documenting the case. This time they wanted it recorded with no chance of being disputed in court. While Xavier was not totally innocent in everything, it became obvious his main concern was to help people like him on the street. He had been used.

The last stop for Vance tonight was in front of internal affairs. Kirkland, the head of the department, closed the door as he pointed to a chair. "I think you know all of this exonerates you. I also know you have a valid suit against the department. I hope we can work it out. What can I do for you?"

"Do you mean aside for ruining my life, and putting me through hell?" While Vance felt some relief, now was the time to put an end to this. "I guess that will do for a start."

"You know you'll be automatically reinstated. That is, if that's what you want."

Vance offered a frozen stare.

"And with full pay for the time you were not working." Kirkland added.

Vance knew this would only be the beginning. "We both know Nelson was not the only one involved in this."

"We plan to do a more complete investigation."

"If I come back, I want to be part of the team conducting this."

"Don't you think you're a little too personally involved with this to do a good job?"

"Do you really think you have a choice?"

"All I can say is that we'll talk."

"Yes, there will be a lot of talking, but I think it will be with whoever replaces you."

"Replaces me?"

"You need to find a good lawyer." Vance pointed to a flash drive. "I have the files you attempted to hide. The ones where you worked with Nelson to have me removed." He spit out the words that he knew would send him into an immediate heart attack. "Listen, you sorry son of a bitch. Does *Black Knight* ring a bell? You're going to jail."

Kirkland raised his head in a cocky stance. "I'm

not sure what you have, but I'll assure you that if it's not obtained legally, it's inadmissible. And to think, at one time Nelson wanted to bring you in to be a part of us."

Vance leaned backwards as he wanted him to further hang himself. "You seem to forget, I was given clearance by a judge to do research, and as such, anything I dig up is very admissible."

Kirkland leaned back in his seat. "You're still wearing a microphone, aren't you?"

"Yep." Vance pointed a finger at him to indicate that he had been tagged.

Moments later, an FBI agent opened the door. "Sir, I think you need to come with me."

As Kirkland stood, the agent indicated for him to turn around. The cuffs fastened quickly. There was no need for additional words as he was escorted out of the room.

Vance lowered his head. It was now over. Well almost.

## Chapter 20

Noella had not slept well the night before. She had worried about Vance, and what he was up to. She could only hope he was safe. Finally, this morning, she learned the details from the FBI. She wanted to call him, but she knew he was probably asleep. He deserved it. He had been telling the truth all the time, he had been framed.

The problem now was trying to explain her father's actions. She knew he did what he thought was best. While he did nothing illegal, he did make it impossible for Vance to discover the truth about what happened to his father. Her father had ordered the destruction of all records that might implicate the firm. In the process, all records of Vance's father were also destroyed. It thus made the tracking of where the gambling losses were paid, and who they were paid to, impossible.

If Vance knew this, he had every right to be mad. What made her proud of Vance the most; however, was how he didn't try to ruin her father or her life in the process. It had to be hard on him. Somehow, she would make it up to him.

Still, how did Vance's father get sucked into the world of gambling? Also, why did no one know anything about it until he committed suicide? She knew Vance would continue his search, and especially with these new revelations. Because of the lapse of the statute of limitations, perhaps even her father could do the right thing this time and help.

Around lunchtime she received a call from Vance. "Hello, Noella. I assume you heard about last night."

"The FBI was here waiting when I got to work. Are you okay? I've been so worried about you."

"For the first time in a long time, I slept very well in my own bed." She heard him chuckle. Good. He appeared to be in a good mood.

"As soon as you feel like it, I need to go with you to see my dad. He has some news for you that I think you deserve."

"If it's about my dad, I'm trying to put that behind me. I have researched it for a long time. Some secrets may need to stay exactly that—secrets."

"I know you have run into a lot of dead ends, but you now have a new door that's open to you. I'll let my father explain it to you."

A long pause indicated that he was thinking about it.

"Please, I owe you this much." Her heart beat fast, as she waited on a response.

"Let me have an hour, and I'll meet you at his office."

"Vance. I love you. Regardless of what you hear, I want you to know that."

"I know you do. We'll talk after we see your father. We have a lot to talk about."

She was hoping he would say he loved her too, but even without words, she knew he did. Allowing him to say it when he was ready would be hard. She hoped he would accept the news her father had, and not walk away from her again.

She picked up her phone and called her dad on his private line. "Dad, I talked to Vance, and he wants to see you in an hour. I hope you're ready for him."

"I've been preparing for this moment for seven years. Thank you for talking him into seeing me."

Vance felt good about being vindicated on charges he used excessive force, and that he had killed innocent people. He knew the prosecutor would push for the death penalty on Nelson's cold blooded murder. It would be a while until life would return to normal, but then again, what would be normal in the future? He still had to go by the police department to answer some questions. It would be interesting to see how they treated him now.

He decided to dress in sports clothes, and look as presentable as he could, especially since he was going to see Noella's father. Later tonight he wanted to spend time with Noella to sort out their lives. The uncertainty of how this would go down made him nervous, but he thought that all might finally be looking up for them. It all depended on what her father had to say. He still wanted to know what the deal was with the Swiss trust company he had located in her dad's pocket.

As he walked into their law office, the receptionist greeted him with a big smile. Apparently she had been put on high alert to make sure he was ushered in to see him. "Mr. Mills, they're waiting for you inside. Can I get you anything to drink?"

"No. I'm fine, thank you."

Once inside, Vance saw her dad sitting behind a large desk. Her dad, in turn, immediately pointed to a small conference table where Noella was waiting for him. She immediately stood and rushed to him. "I'm so glad you're safe. I heard about all the shooting. Are you sure you're not hurt?"

"Yes, I'm fine." He glanced at her father who extended him his hand. "Hello, Sir."

"Sir? Why don't you call me Randy? It is my first name."

Noella moved closer, and hugged Vance. "I'm so sorry for any part in this that I had. I really only wanted to protect you. I couldn't stand to see you get prosecuted. Please forgive me for ever doubting you."

Vance kissed her forehead. He'd never really believed she was truly out to get him. He turned to her father, where he still had doubts.

"Vance, I'm probably the one who needs to beg for your forgiveness the most." Randy settled into one of the chairs at the conference table. "Please have a seat."

Vance moved into the one directly across from him, a confrontation position, but one that felt natural for now. "I'm listening."

Randy reached for a file he had at the end of the table. "When your dad committed suicide, he left us in a very bad situation. We had no idea of how he was getting money for his debts, or if he had taken money from some of the clients we manage. In my haste to cover our position, I ordered many records to be destroyed, those which might implicate the firm. In that haste, I know many records that would give details of your father's activities were destroyed. I'm truly sorry about that."

"I've always thought that details were being hidden from me."

"The truth is, Vance, I still don't know if doing so hurt, or helped the case against him. His fortune disappeared. All indications are that he gambled it away."

"Did you, or did anyone at the firm ever see, or hear about him gambling?"

"While he kept it hidden, there were some records

located where he was gambling. He had been sending large sums of money to an offshore bank."

"If we knew where that bank was, don't you think that it might shed some light on what was going on?"

"Possibly—yes. Unfortunately, those records were destroyed."

"Do you really want to help me?" Vance decided to spread all of his cards on the table.

"Yes, but what can I do?"

"Getting information on the offshore bank account, I think, will never happen. However, I think I know where the parent company is. It is SwissBank. Do you know them?

Endless questions appeared to be floating across his face. "Yes, I know them some. Why do you ask?"

"I found a receipt in your jacket pocket which I borrowed from the boat that had both the offshore banks name on it, and their name."

Noella spoke up, "I gave Vance permission to borrow it when we were on the boat. That's where we hid out for a while."

A brief smile passed Randy's lips. "I won't ask for details, but back to your question. We have set up trust accounts for many clients, and having a Swiss bank account can prove to be very useful. I'm sure your dad used them at times. What are you thinking?"

"I think they may hold the keys to the truth."

"The chance of getting any information from them is next to impossible. Privacy is what they are known for."

"What would we need?"

"To start with you'll need an account number, and a password."

"I have an account number." Vance handed him the account number scribbled on the small piece of paper.

"And what about a password?"

"I can make an educated guess."

"It will be after hours there, but let me see what I can do. We are a good client."

Vance watched him press his intercom button and speak with his secretary to give her instructions to get in touch with the bank. His heart was beating fast. Would it be this simple to learn what happened?

Randy's secretary soon interrupted with the news. A vice-president with a name that didn't register, but who was apparently working for the bank, was on the line. "Hello. It's good to hear from you. How can I be of assistance today?"

"We have a situation here that we need help with. There was an account set up there seven years ago, and I'm not sure if we have the correct account number, or password."

"You know the rules. In order to offer our clients complete privacy, you'll need both."

Vance spoke up. "My name is Vance Mills, and I think this account was set up by my father. Can you check the account number 398684378?"

"And the password?"

"Try vance1004." That was the name his dad had used many times to set up passwords for him when they allowed him to enjoy social media connections.

There was a long pause, as he glanced at Noella's beautiful eyes that were intensely focusing on him.

Finally he returned to the phone. "There is such an account, and the password is correct. The name of the account is Vance trust fund. I heard you say your name was Vance, so my guess is that he had set up a trust account for you."

Vance had a trust fund! The shock made the world disappear into a blur. "I . . . I had no idea. I thought this was an account he used to gamble with!"

"Since you're his son, let me ask you if he's available. We have not heard from him in a long time."

"My father died seven years ago."

"I see. If you can forward me the proper records, the funds can be released to you. There are some minor tax consequences that you might want to see a tax lawyer about, and if possible we would love to meet with you."

Vance felt lost for words. "As you can imagine, this is all new to me."

"I understand, and this happens more than you might realize. I hope you can make arrangements to come see us soon, so we can properly handle the trust for you. To have full access to the funds, you have to be at least twenty-seven."

"I'm thirty now. How much money are we talking about in the trust?"

"Give me a minute, and I'll convert it to dollars for you."

Vance started to ask for privacy, but waited for the answer.

"As of today, this fund has grown to 2,458,234 dollars."

Was it possible to have a heart attack at thirty? His dad did not gamble the funds away. He had built a trust fund with them. Suddenly, he focused on the words *this fund.* "Are there other funds that I need to know about?"

"I knew your father well. I heard you say something about gambling. We were gambling partners at times, but this was always fake money. He was too smart to use real. It was a lot of fun, and you would think he was talking about real money often."

Yes, Vance needed to go see this guy, and soon. He waited for the guy to answer his question which he seemed to be sidestepping.

"All accounts have the same requirements, however. I need an account number for this extra account."

Vance thought hard, and had one guess, for now anyway. "I'm thinking dad would also be thinking of mom. Try an account one number less—398684377 and password Glenda1124." This was his mother's first name and her birthday.

Another long pause. "Amazing! I do have access. This account name is Glenda trust account."

"And the amount in the account?"

"The same."

Vance breathed deeply. His mother would be well taken care of now. He couldn't wait to tell her. It felt hard to contain his emotions.

Randy appeared to understand. "Thank you for your help. You've cleared up some major problems for us."

"I'm glad to be of help. Let me know when you'll be coming to see us, and if I can do anything else."

"You'll definitely be hearing from us." Randy disconnected the call. "Well, I'll be damned."

Vance turned to Randy. "Since he died seven years ago, what will this do to the estate, and any debt he owed?"

"The statute of limitation has run out on it, so there will be no problem to transfer it to you."

He had money. What now? Hot damn! Vance Mills had a lot of money. Another thought suddenly occurred to him—the life insurance on his dad's life. It had been denied due to the suicide. But what suicide? There was no motive, or reason for him to kill himself. He had more research that needed to be done quickly.

He turned to Randy. "I'm now wondering if my dad didn't commit suicide. It appears he had no reason to do so. Can the decision of the insurance company be reopened on new information?"

"The insurance company could allow it, but they do not have to do so. As far as a public relation point of view, however, it will be hard for them to deny the new information. What are you thinking?"

"I really can't speculate until I talk to the forensic guy who investigated my dad's death."

Noella's father acted eager to help. "Let me know what I can do to help."

"I know I'll need a lawyer to help sort through everything. I assume you're available."

"You damn right I am, and at no charge."

"I also have grounds for suit against the police department for unlawful dismissal. They have offered me a settlement already."

"I'm sure you're smart enough to turn that one

down."

"I might not be needing the money, but want to have my name fully restored."

"We'll talk, but refer all offers to me to handle."

"Deal."

"You also need to decide when you can go to Switzerland."

"I guess that depends on when you and Noella are available."

"Why us?"

"I think I need to do something I should have done seven years ago." He glanced at Noella. "It will be hard for you to give away your daughter if you're not there."

Noella edged closer to him. "What makes you think I'll say yes to you?"

"Let's say that I'm giving you some advance warning. I assume you'll need some time to think about it."

"Not really, but I'm curious as to what you have on your mind."

"Listen, I still have a trip I need to make to the Tampa police department. We'll talk later tonight."

"Are you sure you don't want me to go with you?"

"I appreciate it, but this is something I need to do on my own. I need to get to the truth on my dad's death."

"Do you expect more cover-ups?"

"As of right now, I expect them to lean backwards to disclose anything they have."

"Vance, I love you. Please remember that whatever you find out, we can handle together."

"I know, and I'll see you soon. We've a lot to talk about." When he tells her he loves her, he wanted to do it right. Hopefully, that would be right tonight. He had one last truth to obtain. While the police force had fought him on digging for years to find the truth, this time he would not be sidestepped.

### 

Vance walked through the front doors on the police station where he quickly became the center of attention. One officer after another rushed to him, and wanted to shake his hand, or pat him on the back. The threat of a major lawsuit must have circulated quickly.

The crowds around him were too honest to be

staged. Could they really consider him a hero now? Was he considered one of them again? However, did he really want to return to work there? With his newly found fortune, he doubted it. Life would be different, and he needed time to sort it out.

Soon the chief of police joined him. "I know you think we all turned our backs on you, and maybe we did. I hope you'll accept our sincere apology."

Vance smiled. "I'm not one to hold grudges. However, I came here to do two things. I know I need to give a statement on what all happened yesterday."

"Yes, we can do that at your leisure. You're a hero here now." The chief paused for a minute. "You mentioned two things."

"I need to see the complete file on my dad's death, the investigating officer on this case, and the guy in charge of forensics."

"That case was closed seven years ago."

Vance appeared to ignore him. "I also need a private room, and I do mean private."

"Okay, I'll arrange it, but I'd like to know what you're up to."

"The truth."

A detective stepped forward. "The investigating officer was Anderson. I can get him here in a few minutes." The nod from his head indicated he would help Vance any way he could, and without any questions needing to be asked.

The chief glanced at the men lined up behind Vance. "Okay, we owe you. I hope you find what you want."

In less than an hour all had been arranged. Both men sitting in front of Vance appeared nervous, but defiant, almost like they were ready to defend their actions.

Vance started by trying to make them at ease. "I wish we could have had this discussion many years ago. I'm not here to get anyone in trouble, but I do want your help in reconstructing the scene. Can you help me do that?"

They looked slightly more relaxed, but not convinced. "What exactly are you looking for?" Anderson asked.

Vance took the collection of photos from the file he had been given and spread them on the table, as he tried to ignore the fact this was his dad's blood all over the desk and the floor. "Are these all the photos, and do they represent what the scene looked like when you found my dad?"

"It has been a while, but I assume so."

"Let me add one new fact that I have just discovered. My dad did not gamble his money away. He was not in financial difficulty. I want you to look at this scene now in a different light. If suicide was ruled out, what do you see?"

Vance watched both men study the photos. Anderson asked first, "Are you thinking that he was murdered?"

"I also know of no reason that someone would take his life." Vance pointed to the gun. "Is this where you found the pistol?"

"Yes, we were very careful not to move it."

"Is this where you would expect to see it if he shot himself?"

The forensic guy spoke up. "Not exactly. It is several yards out of his grasp."

"Let me ask the question on my mind. If it went off accidentally, how far would the recoil knock the gun from him?"

Neither answered.

"I assume some test would confirm this."

Anderson turned to examine the photos closer. "I can definitely see your point. I think a strong point can be made that it might be an accident. So what are you trying to accomplish?"

"My dad's insurance. On a suicide, the insurance company is not required to pay the claim, on an accident they are. But more than that, I want to clear his name once and for all."

"No promises, but we'll do our best. You do have proof that he was not suicidal."

"Yes, I do."

"It will take a week or two to make this official, but I think we do need to reopen this case.

"Thank you."

## Chapter 21

Noella waited for Vance to arrive at her house. The maid service had cleaned the inside completely, and removed all signs of the attacks on her earlier. While it looked like nothing had ever happened there, the memories returned, as she waited for him.

This house was too big for her, and made her feel lonely for the first time in a while. She had shut out memories of her past. There was no way she could do that now. She needed someone in her life now. She needed Vance.

They still had a lot to talk about. She had her career, and with the money he now has available, his life would be vastly different. She knew that he needed time to consider what he wanted to do. And what was this conversation with her dad about being there to give her away? Did he sneak in a proposal? She raised her hands to her mouth and giggled, which was a sound she hadn't made in years.

When she heard the front bell ring, her heart

raced. It had to be him. While she'd lost him once, she was damn sure not going to allow that to happen again!

Noella opened the door and saw him standing there with a single, red rose. "Hello, beautiful." His voice was smooth, as he focused his attention on her. Their mesmerizing deep-gray color penetrated her soul, and made her freeze.

While she wanted to respond, her voice wouldn't cooperate. He moved closer, as she finally whispered, "I love you, Vance." She reached around his neck and pulled him closer, as she kissed his lips with a passion she simply couldn't control.

The kiss seemed to last forever, but finally she separated slightly from him. As he pulled the door closed behind him, he still offered no words. As a lawyer, she knew how powerful silence could be. With Vance's mastery of timing, he would make a great one.

He paused briefly before he handed her the rose. "I hope you'll accept this single rose as a sign of the first day of the rest of our lives. It may be corny, but I mean it."

"No . . . no, not corny at all. But . . . what life are you talking about?"

"Well, seeing how I already have permission from your father. . . ."

Noella cocked her hip to one side. "—I was wondering about that. I thought you were supposed to propose to the girl first, and with a ring, hint, hint, and get her to say *I do* before you asked her father for permission—"

"Do you mean one of these?" He removed a small box from his pocket. "You know, it's amazing what kind of credit I all of a sudden have at the jewelers."

She went speechless, again.

"You know, we still need to talk, but if you're willing to work out a few things, I think we might be able to get our lives back on track." He kissed her softly before he continued, "What do you think?"

She stuttered as she worked on the right words to say. "I . . . I know your life is all up in the air right now, and I also have some decisions to make."

"I understand." He pressed closer. "All I want to know is if you're willing to compromise, and put us at the top of the list."

This question she did not have to think about. "Absolutely."

"In that case, I think it's time for me to tell you something I think you've known for years."

He lowered to one knee. "Noella, I love you, and have from the first day I met you. You would make me the happiest man on the planet if you would accept this ring, and be my wife." He opened the box and like— wow!

As she froze, he reached for her hand, and slipped it on. "How did you manage to find something so beautiful and huge so fast?"

"I simply asked for the best ring they had. I hope you like it."

"I would have settled for one out of a gum machine, but this is incredible!"

"Does that mean *yes*?"

"Yes, it means yes! I love you very much, Vance."

THE END